The Harlequin

MultiMind

First paperback edition, March 2025
First e-book edition, March 2025
Audiobook edition, March 2025

Cover design by Ejiwa Ebenebe
Edited by Ja'el Knott

ISBN 978-1-952860-14-0 (paperback)
ISBN 978-1-952860-15-7 (ebook)
ISBN 978-1-952860-16-4 (audiobook)

Library of Congress Control Number: 2025900299

www.multimindpublishing.com

Acknowledgement

This book is funded by the Maryland State Arts
Council creativity grant.

Thank you all who had testified, recorded, and took
pictures of what actually happened to the Greenwood
community in Tulsa, Oklahoma.

It wasn't a riot, it was a massacre.
Plain and simple.

Isn't it wild what broke, jealous people do in the
sight of greatness? Mind-blowing, indeed.

Historical Note

This work heavily references the Tulsa Massacre that occurred between May 31 and June 1 in 1921. The town of New Tulsa is fictional but the deadly, race-based massacre referenced is not.

Please take it upon yourselves to read and research about the history of this event. If curious, please scan the QR below to begin.

For Readers of Color, this is not a race pain/race trauma story. There are already so many of those. New Tulsa is just a place where things are different.

Thank you.

<u>Content Warning:</u>

- o References to Historical Prejudice
- o Theme of Abuse (Manipulation)
- o Moderate Blood/Violence
  (Non-Prejudice Based)
- o Mention of Prejudice-Based Violence
  (Non-Graphic)

The Harlequin

Chapter 1

It was a beautiful brisk day in February. The month was nearly over, but winter wasn't. There even was snow on the way late next week — or so they said. The meteorologist always seemed to call for snow on days it would never fall.

New Tulsa was a small, hard-working, port-side town. Borne from the ashes of the horrific and deeply traumatizing Tulsa massacre, New Tulsa had stood the years and decades, protective and self-sufficient. To paraphrase Booker T. Washington, "Put your buckets down where they are, there's diamonds in your own backyard." And that, they truly found in this little Black town. Their own markets, their own businesses. Their own community centers, their own police force. Their own money, their own wealth. The people of Greenwood, Tulsa, the Black community that burned that night from the glaring face of hatred, were quite rich and well-off. So were those who escaped; quite rich but needed a place to be well. Thus rose New Tulsa, a remainder of what was and a proud demonstration of what should forever be, an untouched community fit to flourish. Self-sufficient and glorious.

And right now, this small, glorious town was experiencing a cold snap almost no one could believe.

Rosalyn Davis sat on the windowsill seat of her bedroom. The cushion was plush, flat and velvet. A new one from the holidays gifted to her by her parents, Winston and Demetria. She looked out over the woods and watched the faraway sea that existed off to the distant right, where the grey ocean sloshed against the shore during the reddish-grey sunset. She usually would have a thick book in her lap but she thought to give the e-reader her mother and father bought a try. It wasn't the same but still, Rosalyn had rather try.

Rosalyn was young, freshly seventeen. She had graduated from high school back when she was sixteen — what a feat that was. Her parents saw it as a testament to her will and intelligence; Rosalyn just couldn't take being in school any longer but couldn't live with being a drop-out. So, graduating early it was. She wasn't much of a people person. She was invisible at school, but still didn't want to be there all the same. All the noise, all the people, so much invading reality she didn't want to experience. She was an excellent learner, she just hated school, a secret she had never told her parents. Just graduate early and ask to be a recluse. To which, surprising her, her parents obliged.

All Rosalyn wanted was her books. Her books and their stories. Her distant worlds and fantastical creatures. Fantasy was her home and nature was her comfort. Every day, she would look over the small forest of trees that met her verdant backyard. The wildlife enchanted her, as did all the small adventures she had searching the forest. It always presented her with new follies and discoveries. She would imagine countless tales like the ones she read about. Her imagination comforted her. As did the little forest and the worlds in her books. All she wanted was a soft, gentle life, forever enraptured by the pleasant world of imagination.

Her brother Devonté, on the other hand, was next door in his bedroom gaming his life away. Bouncing in his seat, sometimes yelling (which would be quickly shushed by the parents downstairs), rapturously clutching his blue camouflage controller, Devonté collected countless kills with his buddies online. The basking console that sat next to his clear-case computer tower under his desk was a bit new, a gift for immaculate grades from mom and dad. No community college was hard for him, including the one he went to, Mary McLeod Bethune Community College. It was just an easy stroll of a pit stop before college proper. Nevertheless, Devonté never turned down a new console of any kind.

Brilliant and dotted with a series of glowing colors in a thin strip along the onyx side, the console was the newest drop, the Lawson 970 series. Top graphics, seamless portability with an accompanied handheld travel set (limited editions only), and it also doubled as a wi-fi gateway. To top it all off, it had a massive online game store that made competitors blow steam. Devonté kept the holographic sticker that came with the new console, slapped on the computer monitor cubby wall of his desk:

"Behold the Invention of Modern Fun ... Are You Ready, Player One?"

His mom told him to really appreciate the Lawson, it was not easy to get. Winston nearly had to rip one out of the hands of the weakest looking teenager he could find until a store worker told him there was a limited edition in the back, newly arrived. It was a hundred dollars more but it also wasn't having to snatch a console out of the hands of an unsuspecting kid — who also turned out to have a very hawkish father as well. Getting to the register was a near bloodbath when the other parents and teens noticed what he had.

At least the e-reader he also got that day with his wife was easy to get. Way easier.

Devonté played almost every day, either alone or with his virtual crew, P0p.killa, N0.nonsense and Beepz. They were longtime friends, joined by their love of gaming and digital adventure. He had known them for years, though he only had met them a few times in-person at anime and comic conventions. They would ship each other gifts and drops from time to time, though. As far as Devonté was concerned, they were some of the best friends he'd ever had.

Downstairs, the parents enjoyed a nice, crackling fire going in the living room fireplace under the wide flat-screen television and a bold statue of the Black Panther on the white brick mantle. They snuggled together on the couch after a bustling day of work. Demetria was the lead supervisor of the camera repair and picture restoration store downtown; Winston was a head delivery manager at a port-side warehouse in northern New Tulsa. Both loved their jobs, they paid well and had wonderful benefits. Not at all much like the awful jobs that lived outside of New Tulsa, which were filled with glass ceilings and prejudiced hiring committees that would regularly say "you're not the right fit" — unless you wanted a menial job with low wages. Silly rules over hair and it seemed like the same kind of person got hired almost everywhere: anyone but everyone who looked like Demetria & Winston. Again, unless you wanted menial jobs with low wages.

In New Tulsa, there were plenty of jobs, including the burgeoning technology quadrant blossoming downtown, Wonder City. Called "The Golden Chocolate City", or "the town of self-secluded buppies" by surrounding locals, New Tulsa made sure to look out for its own and its own alone. The town never cared about what others called them. New Tulsa firmly believed that good fences made for great neighbors. And strong walls made for lasting generations that *wouldn't* fall to flames and terror. Never again. No projects, no hoods, crack never happened and there hadn't been a single massacre since. Nothing wrong with wanting to be an exception when everyone else would be infected.

And this is what Winston and Demetria enjoyed, wrapped up snug on their couch, cuddled together as they discussed their plain lives in their plain town. Exactly what they wanted and were raised to desire by their parents and grandparents, who fought hard and toiled harder to make the town what it was today. The Sankofa bird stood on the town's crest and flag for a reason. As was the town's motto on their seal: Heshima, Utukufu, Maisha; "Honor, Glory, Life".

Winston and Demetria spoiled their kids, they knew it. But what was the point of working hard if one couldn't provide even occasional pops of joy? They were well off enough that they could treat their kids' whimsies as needs: Devonté loved games, Rosalyn loved books. Neither engaged in atrocious behaviors, like the outsiders around them, and they both worked hard for their whimsies. Take Rosalyn, she graduated from Wells Academy early at sixteen and with honors. They saw how hard Rosalyn worked to obtain that. She wanted a year or so off to decompress and simply be? Sure, she could start college when she turns eighteen.

Besides, Winston and Demetria remembered their college experiences, both outside of New Tulsa. Actually, that was how and where they met. Neither of them were any too interested in mailing her off to that world too early. They knew Rosalyn lived inside her head too much, always stuck in a dream world. All it would take is one No-Good with honeyed words to pull their precious daughter into a world of trouble and misery. As Winston would put it, "All boys want at that age is to seek and destroy. Seek and *destroy*."

They wanted to give Rosalyn some time to get out of her head and her shell before college. At least learn that there is a time and a place for fantasy and a time and a place for reality. Thankfully, they lived in New Tulsa, that was all they had to teach. The outsiders had it worse. So, they didn't mind waiting.

And then there was their nineteen-year-old son, Devonté. Demetria and Winston thought video games were only for kids but he simply couldn't put the controller down. And, oh, "e-sports". How sitting at a controller could be on par with an actual sport was beyond them. But the prized tournaments Devonté had won downtown at the BLM Community Centre were massive and lucrative, so Demetria and Winston were willing to accept *that* much. However, Demetria and Winston also knew Devonté had a tendency to forge friendships with outsiders. They have even heard him talk fondly about them, as if they were brothers.

That part concerned Demetria and Winston. To survive, one has to stay an exception, that was the spirit of New Tulsa. Everyone else on the outside was seen as crabs in a bucket. Winston and Demetria had rather their son only befriend other New Tulsans but they tried not to mind that he had friends in places like Chicago and Detroit. Tried. From time to time, the very thought of all the things the outsiders could mentally infect their son with would riddle them with shivers. But, all the same, they tried to allow it. If he brought an outsider home as a relationship, though … perhaps they could allow it — as long as the outsider assimilated quickly into the New Tulsan ways. Winston and Demetria didn't care if it was a boy or girl, that hadn't been a concern since Stonewall played out on their televisions and scared the people of New Tulsa into worrying that they were finally becoming just like the outsiders. Demetria and Winston just wanted to be sure the person could adjust and leave their undesirable outsider ways where it should be: on the outside of New Tulsa, where it belonged.

Bad enough Winston had to explain to Devonté how to interact with officers outside of New Tulsa. "They're not like the officers we have here, son," he would remind him. "Besides, whatever you need already lives here. We got diamonds in our own backyards, why go digging for other people's zircon?" If only they could shield Devonté and Rosalyn forever. At least they had home.

"Babe, did you put too much ice in my drink again?" asked Demetria. Her soda tasted watery and every sip was like drinking from a chilly lake of ice floes. Her dark mahogany face crinkled as she examined her glass. Half full, chunked with ice and brisk to the touch.

Winston surveyed the cup as well, "I thought you liked a lot of ice," he pouted. His face was round, different from his wife's angular face, and he had pitch copper skin. They both had wide noses and plump lips but he had significant dimples and thinning hair he desperately tried to retain. At least his wife still had her plump, royal crown of thick, dark hair, twisted up and pinned up.

"Not when it's a billion degrees below, honey," Demetria lamented. If it were summer she would have been fine. Even delighted. But during the cold snap? Overkill.

Winston offered, "How about hot cocoa instea—"

"Get the shot!" ruptured from upstairs. "Don't worry about me! Just kill the shot, man! Beepz got me—"

"*Devonté*!", boomed Winston over his shoulder from the couch at the cream stairwell to the second floor.

Silence.

Demetria stared baffled over her shoulder at the stairwell that sat on the other side of the living room far behind them. How those games always got her son so wound up forever made her wonder.

Though Winston got his silence, he still demanded, "Calm it *down*! You ain't in a real war, *boy*!"

"Sorry, Dad!" yelled Devonté.

Winston sighed and rubbed his head in wonder. Some days he questioned if nearly getting trampled and tackled for that Lawson was worth it. "That boy is *always* on that game!" he gruffed. "What is it? *Super Happy Massacre 4*? Always yellin' and shootin'. I mean, I remember the first Lawsons when I was a young boy. I loved my Jerry 8000 — but this ... we didn't have all the violent games—"

"I remembered you playing Death Force when we got together," Demetria reminded. She sat down her watery soda in the cup holder of the couch's arm rest and laid herself against her husband, arm draped over his stomach. He had a potbelly but he wasn't portly. At least not yet, a work in progress since he started having kids. She still held her thin figure but that was moreso genetics, and the fact she hardly had a proper moment to catch a decent bite to eat at work due to all the bustling she had to do to make sure everything and everyone worked to expectations. She remembered when he was more strapping then, but she liked him more snuggly now.

"And I remember borrowing the game from *you* when you got the Lawson 860," Winston clarified with a knowing smile. He laid his head upon her fluffy crown and exhaled, "The boy betta not turn out violent and crazy—"

"We didn't," Demetria pointed out. She remembered how lackadaisical Winston used to be — then he had a boy. Between national tragedies and nutty outsider police officers, Winston became a little more uptight about everything. Even New Tulsa occasionally saw pops of problems. And *that*, was indeed a problem. Demetria, however, always tried to be his counterbalance.

Winston gruffed some more, "We didn't because our games didn't simulate murder in 4k. I 'on't know, babe—"

"No, no, *no!*" raged again from upstairs. "We didn't get Play Star of the Game? How? How didn't we get Play—"

"*Devonté!*" Winston roared over his shoulder once more. "One more *time!*"

"He means it!" Demetria boomed beside him. "Keep it down, your sister is trying to *read!*"

After a small moment of silence, Devonté called back, "Sorry, Rose! Sorry, everybody!"

Both Demetria and Winston sighed. They snuggled up together again in attempt to resume their *quiet* evening.

"Lord, please keep me from killing this boy," Winston prayed as he laid his head down once more upon his wife's crown.

Demetria hummed in agreement as she threaded an arm over his stomach once more and nuzzled into his cheek.

Just another night in the Davis' house.

Soon, night fell and all was quiet. Everyone was in bed, except for Rosalyn. She wanted to read by the bright moonlight. Rosalyn always found it so ethereal to curl up and read by the silvery light of the radiant moon. She even would keep track of the night weather and moon phases on her phone to ensure maximum reading pleasure. She did it so well she could eyeball the dates of the next phases with just a glance at the sky. She could tell when night would fall almost to the minute, the likely cloud cover, everything. It brimmed her with such joyous delight to anticipate her moonlight readings every time they came near. Just her, the moon, the stars and the calm world. She never had out her e-reader for her moonlight sessions, too distracting. Paper books only.

The moonlight bathed her dark skin in gentle silver radiance. Her ivory nightgown seemed almost illuminated in comparison to her skin. Her poufy, fluffy hair was bound up in a nicely wrapped ivory-gold bonnet, a feat carried out by her mother earlier that day. Rosalyn didn't like bonnets; she already had a satin pillow covered in happy flowers and polka dots but her mother always tried to instill beauty methods in her. Over and over, Demetria would remind her, "There eventually will come a day you'll be somewhere that has pillows that aren't good for your hair. Better to know it and never need it than to need it and not know it." So, Rosalyn would let her mother wrap up her hair whenever she saw fit. At least it wasn't visiting the salon. Rosalyn hated that.

The salon seemed to always teem with loud and chattering women, in Rosalyn's eyes. Rosalyn simply wasn't one of them. Her mother was, on the other hand. The ladies were nice, just … invasive. And how they invaded her reading. At the salon, Rosalyn sat in the same chair her mother sat in since she herself was a little girl. Her fluffy, voluminous hair was cared for by the same woman who worked on her mother's hair since adolescence, Mrs. Barbra. Mrs. Barbra owned the salon with her wife, Mrs. Deonah for decades. Beforehand, it was owned by Mrs. Deonah's mother, Sallie, who passed it onto Deonah as a wedding gift to her daughter and a retirement gift to herself.

Mrs. Barbra eventually learned how to let Rosalyn be when she sat in her chair but sometimes Deonah loved to ask questions and "bring Rosemary out of her shell". Mrs. Deonah always called Rosalyn "Rosemary", simply because she found the name pretty. Demetria found it heartwarming to have her shy child nicknamed by a community elder but Rosalyn didn't feel one way or the other, she just wanted to be home with her books.

Demetria knew her daughter hated being anywhere but on her sill under the moon with a good book, but the salon visits were little tries to have her daughter out and about in the community. At least while they lived in a community safe enough to do so. If Demetria had the lives of her distant aunts and uncles outside of New Tulsa, then she would have done everything she could to keep her gentle and soft daughter home. She knew how the world treated Black girls, she even experienced it first hand when she traveled away for college. It was not the New Tulsa way.

Sometimes, Demetria made Rosalyn volunteer at the bookstore or library. If volunteer slots weren't available, there was the BLM Community Centre, where there was always something to do.

The BLM Community Centre was new. There wasn't as much of a major need for the activists in New Tulsa like there was everywhere else so they basically served as the sleeping reserves in case things got hairy elsewhere — and *especially* before it could hit New Tulsa's shores. It was a community center, a job center for both training and procurement, a place for children to play, a place for elders to relax away from home, and for those who wanted to find fun things to do. The center was the first to soak the small town in video game tournaments and virtual reality arcades.

Rosalyn was a little scared of the girls and boys there. They were all so bubbly, hyper and chipper, and she … just wanted to be to herself. Rosalyn knew her mother would give the center permission to drag her into their reindeer games at any given opportunity, bare or abundant. She also knew it was her mother's kind-hearted attempt to make her a little more social, nothing nefarious, so she would try to stick it out the best she could. At least the girls and boys weren't mean, just over-friendly.

But tonight, it was just Rosalyn. Alone in person but not in spirit, she had a lovely new fantasy book to accompany her. This time, it was an enchanting story of a boisterous Forest King who annoyed the rest of the forest with his ego and antics. The Flower Queen and King together concocted a plan to send him on an adventure to request parlance with a mountain king that did not exist — not to rid of the Forest King for his land but merely to gather a desperately needed break (although, an "unfortunate" demise would not have been too unwelcomed, either) — but the Forest King was too full of himself to know, notice, or care if the mountain king was real. There was an adventure to be had.

The story delighted Rosalyn. It was the newest book in the series, her mother was quick to nab a copy as fast as she could in that holiday rush as Winston fought the video game crowds. A signed copy at that. Demetria had to jostle with many book lovers for that, one even tried to bite her and another attempted to slip the signed book off her gift pile when she checked a message on her phone while in line for the register. Rosalyn didn't care that it was signed, only that it was here.

Rosalyn looked outside her window when a spate of clouds masked the moon briefly as they sailed past. How enchanting the night sky looked, with all its beautiful stars, wispy clouds and a glowing moon's radiance. This was what she lived for.

What she nearly missed was a curious figure down at the edge of the forest line in her backyard. Usually, Rosalyn would spot bunnies or even deer walking in the snow-covered backyard but this time, it was a strange figure. A man. A man dressed in a white jester-like outfit. Dark hued diamonds patterned up his legs and spotted his buttoned-up overcoat. His head was half covered with a dual horned jester's cowl that revealed the lower half of his face. He had plain white, concave outlines with gold lining for eyes, he had no true eyes to speak of. His face was long, dark skinned, and with a pointed black beard. His smile was toothy and wide. The figure raised a white gloved hand that bore long, tapered claws that beckoned Rosalyn to come outside, to join them in the forest.

A harlequin? thought Rosalyn. She only had seen them in books and imagined them in her head … but this one seemed real. And alluring.

With eager haste, Rosalyn left her window seat and pulled off her bonnet to let out her magnanimous cloud of jet-black hair. It had a neat center part and poured past her shoulders. She went to her bed to slip on her fluffy, dust brown slippers. Rosalyn placed down her book, face down and parted on the page she was on, and fled her room.

The house was silent and sturdy, almost nothing creaked as Rosalyn padded down the stairs and through the kitchen behind the stairwell to head outside into the chilly, snowy backyard.

The air was brisk; the cold gripped her bones through her long nightgown. She should have gone back inside for her coat but she instead wanted to push forward and thus tried to ignore the cold. Instead, she tried to focus on the harlequin figure that just turned around and disappeared as he walked into the forest.

The dappled moonlight sprinkled through the snow-covered branches. The snow improved visibility from the reflected moonlight but still, Rosalyn couldn't see anyone or anything for yards.

Go deeper, the wind softly whispered. *Find me deeper.*

And deeper Rosalyn went, fully consumed by the forest.

The snow tinkered down and landed in her hair as she passed underneath the branches. A small grin started to slide upon her cold face as she traveled deeper into the woods. She carefully stepped over fallen branches as the deep, snowy ground cover softly crunched underfoot. The cold still consumed her, she even had a visible shiver but she was consumed with a greater determination to find the curious harlequin more. At least to see if it wasn't a dream. She did, however, promise herself that if she got to the river in the woods and still found nothing, she would hustle back inside to the warmth, hot cocoa and her books.

The snow twinkled in her hair but her hair was thick enough that most of it did not touch her scalp, except near the part. Rosalyn tried to ignore the occasional pricks of chill to her head on her neat part.

Her breath plumed out as her thin body rattled from the digging cold. Rosalyn wanted to call out to the figure but didn't know what to say. Besides, her teeth were too busy chattering as she pursued deeper and deeper into the woods.

Rosalyn stopped at a small clearing, frigid, shivering and alone.

Before she could wonder once more if she did indeed see anything and whether it was her over-active imagination or not, out came a deep, nearby voice.

"My, my, who is this girl with the stars in her hair?"

The figure she saw from her window appeared. He gazed upon her with an adoring smile. He couldn't help but bask in her radiance.

The clearing they stood in somehow warmed up, at least around Rosalyn. Her shivering fell away, her chattering teeth stilled. There she stood, amazed but never frightened. Rosalyn was too taken in by the figure to feel any fear.

The figure continued, aghast in their own wonder and gracious luck, "My, does this night finally come to seek me? Usually, it is we who chase the moon and the stars. Rarely the other way around. What favor have I been shown, to be so lucky?"

Rosalyn blushed and tilted her head away with a coy smile. She always was terrible with kind approaches. Even worse with harsh approaches but New Tulsa had few of those. That was an outsider's thing.

The harlequin figure tilted their head to get a better look at her bashful face. He couldn't help but adore her. Her magnificence astounded him, as did her delicate ways. Captivated, the figure approached her a step or two, star-struck in his words and his gait.

"Midnight Maiden. What a ravenous beauty you are," the bells in his cowl tinkered as he spoke. "With skin like the night sky, hair like the clouds, glittered with stars. Please, I must." The harlequin presented to Rosalyn a deep and gracious kneel in the snow before her. The small bells on the tip of his horns and at the end of his crimson, curled shoes gently tinkered among his movements and words. "Forgive me, if you will, for not doing this sooner. I simply was too taken in by your capturing sight."

Rosalyn didn't know what to do. All she could do was smile, completely enamored and swept away by his warm words. She had always dreamed of a fairytale prince to come visit her, even the Forest King she read about enchanted her. And now, here was a princely figure bowing to her in the snow, awestruck by her. She couldn't help but to smile.

The harlequin stood up. No snow stuck to him, nor did he leave tracks. He remained beaming, tall and beautiful.

"Again, I must ask, who is this pretty girl with the stars in her hair? What luck finds me that I should be happened upon by such a graceful and lovely creature. Of wit, of beauty, oh how she is magnificent. Again, I must state she is as beautiful as midnight herself. Her skin, that I already adore, is the glorious sky that watches over us. Her splendid hair is as light and stupendous as the clouds that sail above us — And look!" The harlequin reached out a wanting, rattling hand towards her hair but never dared to touch, "Look at how they hold the stars so delicately. So … so *magnificent*! What honor to be given by the ever-mysterious goddess of the night to have one of Her many daughters stand before me." The harlequin snatched his hand back and threw his eyes askance as his clawed fingers loosely covered his mouth. "Forgive me, I probably spoke too much. I couldn't help the words that sailed out of me." He looked back at Rosalyn, almost visibly unsure.

Rosalyn blushed, dumbfounded and charmed.

The harlequin walked up to Rosalyn slowly, "Do you grace me because …." He gently brushed his clawed hands over her glittering hair and brought the sharp tips of his spindly fingers together in front of his chest to pull them apart. A delicate necklace made of fallen snow drops spun from between his fingers like a single strand of spider thread, dotted with crystal droplets. A significant droplet hung down as the pendant. "Is it that you wish to be mine? To be the radiant sun to your glorious night? I would love you and cherish you forever to the end of time. Even beyond. Please, *please* give me your mercy and say you'll be mine."

Rosalyn stared at the beautiful necklace. She had never seen one so beautiful and captivating before. And to be given to her in such an enchanting way? Rosalyn looked at the necklace, then at the harlequin, and soon back at the necklace. Her head was empty from awe but her heart couldn't help but to swoon.

"Please, dear maiden," implored the Harlequin. "Your skin is the night; I wish to be wrapped up in it." He smiled broadly and hung the necklace over her head.

With a gentle nod, Rosalyn whispered, "Yes." She closed her eyes and waited to accept the necklace.

An adoring but cruel smile brightened on the harlequin's face as he lowered the necklace down over Rosalyn's head and placed it around her neck. As he cleared her hair from beneath the necklace, it shrank closely to her neck, almost like a loose choker. The pendant droplet glittered like a star.

The harlequin bent to her ear and whispered, "I'll be yours for as long as you'll be mine, Midnight Maiden."

Chapter 2

The rest of the week was odd for Rosalyn, it was almost like she couldn't feel it pass by. She remembered being scooped up by the harlequin after he gave her the necklace and delivered her back to her bed, safe, warm and sound. After that, everything else was a blur. She laid in bed day and night wondering if that night was real. And every time she wondered, she would touch her necklace, which felt like a delicate crystal under her fingertips. The pendant glittered passionately when she examined it in the bathroom mirror.

Rosalyn spent every night searching for the harlequin in the forest but regularly came back empty handed and a bit broken-hearted. Search all night, sleep all day, that was her life. They met on a Wednesday night, but Rosalyn worried by Friday night that maybe she had done something wrong. That the Harlequin was waiting for an offering or something she didn't know she had to give. Rosalyn figured the answer lived online but she didn't want to look anything up, to invite the brute world into her wonderful fantasy with its harsh words and ridiculing commentary.

Her family, on the other hand, wondered what spurred this change in Rosalyn.

Devonté asked late Saturday afternoon over jollof take-out at the dinner table in the kitchen, "'Ey, y'all noticed Rose is a little … vampirey recently? Like she don't be around, except at night?" He picked at his fragrant side dish of potatoes and carrots on his iron red plate before having a few bites. The kitchen shared space with the dining area, which sat behind the living room. A thin brass bar divided the marble tiled dining area floor from the cream tan living room carpet. The kitchen and dining area spanned the width of the house, lined with its black mahogany cabinets and black marble countertops. The ironwood dining table sat on the right-hand side. The plain white door to the backyard sat on the left, behind the second-floor stairwell and opposite of the closed oakwood door to the basement.

At the dining table, piles of ripped open paper bags, clear plastic cups filled with food and styrofoam containers sat in the center of the circular table. The ivory orbed lights above basked the area in a crisp, cool glow.

Demetria cleared her throat over her small plastic takeout cup of dumpling soup. "Firstly, it's 'she *isn't* around—'"

"Thank you," Winston grumbled as he picked with an ox-tail.

"—and secondly, she does seem a little off. But maybe it's another book crush — wait, wait," Demetria paused as she held up her hands. "Isn't the moon full this week or something? She usually stays up late during those."

Devonté wasn't buying it. "Ma, she's like a zombie or something. Like, a night zombie or something. She 'on't usually act like this." Something was definitely off in his sister, he was certain of that.

Demetria waved it off, "You know she gets book crushes from time to time—"

"Remember her Luke Youngblood phase?" Winston snickered.

Demetria couldn't help but to laugh, "Ahhhh, I remember. *Harry Potter*. He played the Jordan boy who would do the Quidditch matches. Ohhhhh, don't remind me. Her bubble was popped when she saw him on *Community*."

"'*Pop-pop!*'" Winston mimicked with a bit of a false falsetto before breaking off into laughter. Demetria guffawed harder at his impression as he smiled, "The first boy I gotta console her about is one on TV. I'm tellin' ya, what a time to be alive." He went back to his ox-tails, still tittering to himself. He had half a plate left and worked steadfast.

Devonté was the only one not laughing. He remembered how broken hearted she was from the character break. If anything, it showed him how deep inside her own head she could plunge. She reminded him of his gaming buddy who lived in the East End of London that sank pound after pound on a Vocaloid character until he found himself crushed under heavy debt. Now, his buddy's gaming name, StrikeD34th, hardly ever lit up on his friends list anymore. StrikeD34th rarely replied to pings and requests either.

"Ma, Dad, I'm just sayin'. Rose seems a little off," shrugged Devonté. He had almost finished his plate, only ox-tail bones and some fish remained.

Winston shrugged back, "Well, go bring her down here. Before the food gets cold."

"You mean 'before I eat it all'," Demetria ribbed.

Winston chuckled as he reached for more jollof to shovel out of the clear container with his bamboo takeout spoon, "That too."

Devonté headed out the dining room, mildly annoyed to be unheard, and went into the living room to bound up the stairs.

The top floor hallway beamed brightly from the cool white rail lights above. The walls were all white, they matched downstairs. Rosalyn and Devonté's cherrywood doors stood side by side, both closed. Down the hallway sat several other doors, all closed except for the bathroom. The closed door at the very end of the hall led to the master bedroom, where the parents slept. The other closed doors, including the door between Devonté's room and the bathroom, were closets. The bathroom was dark and opened just a tad. The upstairs carpet was particularly plush, thanks to the power cleaning Winston did last summer.

Devonté knocked on his sister's door.

No response.

He knocked again, a little harder this time.

Again, no response.

He rapped on the door once more and called out, "'Ey, sis. Rose! Food's downstairs. We got jollof, fish and ox-tail from the Happy Trout place you like."

Still no answer.

Devonté cracked open the door a peek, "Rozay?"

Rosalyn laid fast asleep, bundled in her peach comforters. Her room was a typical teenager's room, if it lived in a library. Every surface had a book on it. At least a stack of books, if not stacks of books. Next summer was going to be the Basement Bookshelf project, where part of the basement would be remodeled to house all her books and give her some much-needed space in her bedroom. Devonté's room was almost as cluttered but with games and a bigger, full-size bed.

Devonté went over to her small, twin sized bed and rocked the sleeping lump awake. "Rozay, food downstairs. From your fav—"

"Harley?" Rosalyn bumbled out as she cleared the covers from her head and stared up desperately. No harlequin, just Devonté.

She looked down, crestfallen.

Deep book crush, guessed her brother. He looked around her room, how she sank so deep into these worlds was beyond him. Books weren't much his thing, games were. But he could understand being smitten over a character. He never forgot how much he was enraptured by Shuri but Storm was his first love. He had even spent his first big tournament check on a magnificent Storm statue in all her thunderous glory. Cost him almost a whole grand but it was one of his most treasured purchases. The statue sat on its own shelf, surrounded by his collection of

Storm comic books. His Black Panther statue lived downstairs. Devonté would have had the Black Panther statue in his room, it wasn't cheap either and, thus, deserved a proper display— but, hey, competition.

Devonté sighed and shook his little sister a little more, "Nope, Devonté. Ma and Dad got food for you downstairs."

Rosalyn shuffled under the covers and whined. Where was her harlequin?

"I know, I know," commiserated her brother. He sang, "Back to life, back to reality." In his regular bass tone, he consoled, "He'll still be here waiting for you after you get something to eat. You can bring your book down with you if you want. Dad's burnin' through the ox-tails so you may wanna move fast."

Rosalyn shuffled about some more as Devonté unfurled her from her covers. She wore her necklace under her nightgown, where no one really noticed the occasional corner glint when she would turn her head about.

"Come on, sleepyhead," Devonté urged gently.

Rosalyn got up and slumped onto her brother. Her stomach gave a bit of a soft rumble. She didn't even remember if she had a decent meal recently.

"Did Dad get the pineapple soda?" she grogged out.

"Already destroyed it," Devonté smirked. He rubbed his head, it was almost time to get another line up. He made a mental note to pit stop at the barber after class tomorrow. He rubbed his broad nose, a feature he shared with his parents and sister. And they both had their parents' smile, which they shined at each other as they headed downstairs.

"There's the star of the show!" crowed Winston as he sat perched on his stool at the dinner table, another ox-tail in hand. "Come on so your mother doesn't blame me for eating all the food!" He spun around on his stool and continued eating. Demetria rolled her eyes as she worked on some fish.

"Kids," she declared, "this man eats like a tornado. You all get yourselves something. Devonté, make your sister a plate. Rosie, don't forget, hairdresser and book club tomorrow." Before Rosalyn could get out a complete pout, Demetria pointed, "Uh-uhn. No sad faces, little missy. You got to get some social skills in before you head to college. You're almost seventeen and a half. We won't push you to college until eighteen but we didn't say we would let you stay in your room for almost two entire years." Demetria softened a bit, she saw Rosalyn start to shrink into herself, "You'll love it, honey. So many girls like you there." Demetria sighed, sometimes she wished Rosalyn didn't inherit so much of her determination and stubbornness. "Rosie, one visit. One visit, please?" begged Demetria. "If you hate it, we won't make you go. Can we agree on that?"

Rosalyn still pouted as Devonté layered on the last pieces of ox-tail he pulled from his father's plate but she reluctantly agreed. "Okay," she acquiesced in a whisper.

Devonté fished a bamboo fork out of one of the biggest bags and gave it to her sister. He decided to change the subject. "Sleepin' like the dead, huh? That book you readin' must be pretty good," he ribbed. Devonté hoped to get something out of her. Especially in front of the parents. Something was off and he knew it.

Rosalyn almost didn't know what he was talking about until she connected the dots in her head. "Oh, yeah. I love the book so far," she half-lied. She really did love her

Forest King book but she hadn't continued it since she met the harlequin. Too busy looking for him.

Winston sighed into a breathy chuckle. Every time he would wonder why he had such an odd daughter, he would then remind himself that this was the *worst* he was facing, whereas fathers on the outside experienced *far* worse. What luck, even in New Tulsa.

To his youngest, Winston suggested, "That's fine and all but could you try reading by the *sun*light for a little while? Got your brother thinking you'll bite him in his sleep—"

"Nah nah, I ain't say all 'lat," Devonté defended. "I said she was staying up at night and sleeping during the day like a vampire—"

"Vlah, vlah!" mocked Winston in a terrible Transylvanian accent, his hands poised like claws. "It is I, Count Blackula! Ah von't to suck your blood!" Winston found himself a riot. He even patted his belly as his smile lines creased all over his face.

Demetria rolled her eyes again but couldn't help but to crackle out a small roll of laughter she tried to keep in. Devonté rubbed his face in second-hand embarrassment. Rosalyn tried to laugh it off but she wondered where was her harlequin.

Chapter 3

Nighttime fell. All in the house were asleep, except for Rosalyn. She was out in the chilly, frozen woods. The snow hadn't melted even a little yet, too cold to. The moon still shone brightly, though not nearly as full as it began to wane. All the same, Rosalyn tried to use the lesser light to follow her previous footsteps in the snow. She had to strain her eyes somewhat but she still could make out the depressions.

"Harlequin?" she softly called. "It's-it's your mid-Midnight Maiden." Her voice shook from the cold and the creeping fear that this was all somehow fake. She pulled out her necklace from under her lace collar and thumbed it. It didn't glow, point, nothing. She thought it would all come to her like it did in her books but she felt and knew nothing new or different.

"Harlequ—"

"Is that your name for me, precious Midnight Maiden?" asked the harlequin behind her.

She jumped around in surprise.

Nothing.

"My most delicate," the harlequin whispered into her ear, again from behind. She could feel him leaned against her back. She turned around to face him saying, "Is 'Harlequin' your name for me?" He had a broad, comforting smile.

Rosalyn nodded. It didn't dawn on her to ask if he had a particular name. She just went through with her assumption, maybe that's why he never came to see her—

"I am most enchanted that you granted me a precious and loving name." He backed up to bow sincerely to her. "I shall forever be known as your precious 'Harlequin', my beautiful Midnight Maiden." He rose and stepped close to her once again, "It does not escape me that you called for me, over and over again." He looked away, his parted claws covering his face, "Please forgive me, my precious and beautiful Midnight Maiden. The wonderful goddess should not gift me one of Her immaculate daughters and I have nothing fitting to show or give her." He looked again at Rosalyn, whose cheeks grew hot from blushing, "You gave me your heart, the least I could do is give you something fitting in return. But ... before I digress ...." Something troubled the Harlequin in his tone but he still kept a pleasant smile, "Who was that sire you leaned against as he plucked you from the bed I rested you in? Is he one I should worry of?"

At first, Rosalyn stood there, baffled and lost. Then, it dawned upon her. She brightened with an alleviated smile, "That's my brother, Devonté. He was just waking me up—"

"Perhaps I should wake you from henceforth," suggested the Harlequin. "Precious Midnight Maiden, you are my gift and I am unworthy to have you, I know, but …" he stroked her soft, cold cheek with the knuckles of his claws, "It is my duty to you, or may the goddess curse me and give you to him. I do not want that."

Before Rosalyn could object or say otherwise, the Harlequin kissed her. It was her first ever kiss. She had never imagined it would occur so suddenly. It felt … nice. Warm. Gentle and sincere. The kiss tasted of pine and sweets.

The Harlequin broke the kiss and Rosalyn felt a bit of a head rush. Before she could sink to the ground, the Harlequin dropped to a kneel and caught her. She sat on his knee and slumped against his shoulder.

He smiled at her, "My dear maiden, are you okay?"

Rosalyn grinned at him, blushing and woozy.

The Harlequin bent over and kissed her again. Warmth radiated within her. The Harlequin then dotted kisses on her neck. He made sure to kiss the pendant he gave her. He then snuck a last kiss onto her heart. The last kiss surprised her most, she felt good but she didn't want to go that far. However, she was in too much of a mixture of emotions to say so.

Laid in his arms and upon his knee, the Harlequin looked over Rosalyn adoringly. He gave a soft brush to her cheek. Rosalyn gazed back at him with a silly grin. She reached up to touch his face—

And she woke up in her bed again. It was morning. Rosalyn wracked her brain for her last memories. The best she could piece together was the Harlequin laying her down in her bed and wishing her good night. Her lips still ebbed with the shadow of his kisses, as did her neck. And her heart, which the thought of it made it flutter and she blushed deeply.

Her first kiss.

And it was as magical as she would hope it would be.

Rosalyn couldn't help but to smile like a buffoon.

She looked for any signs that the Harlequin woke her all around her room. All seemed normal until she noticed she felt the shadow of a new kiss on her hand and cheekbone. She grasped her cheek and blushed harder.

Rosalyn wanted to hop out of bed and head into the woods but there was a rap at the door.

"Rosie," Demetria called. She knocked again. "Gotta get up, sleepyhead. Hair and book club today. Gotta get ready, Rose."

That snapped Rosalyn back to earth. She dove under her covers to hide her blushing and silly smile. Rosalyn called back, "Okay, Ma!"

Under her covers, Rosalyn heard a whisper, *Oh, Midnight Maiden, is this how much you love the dark?*

Rosalyn threw back the covers. She found nothing but some satin pillows and an empty bed. She then felt another phantom kiss against her neck. Wooziness overcame her and she fell off to sleep again, hitting the pillow with a sound plop.

"Rosie! *Rosalyn!* Rosie, get up!" Demetria rattled her daughter awake. *Teenagers, I swear,* fumed Demetria.

Rosalyn cracked open her eyes. She was greeted by an irritated and almost roaring mother. She felt groggy, like she woke up from the deepest sleep. There were more phantom kisses on her lips as she tried to gain her senses. She could taste pine and sweets.

"Rosie, c'mon and get up!" Demetria lamented. She sighed angrily, "Mrs. Barbra does *not* do late and you know that. Get dressed, put on a hat and let's *go*." She gruffed, "Tryna sneak in a quick cat nap. Your dad said don't stay up so late! You know you had this!"

Rosalyn got up, bleary and confused. She then plopped back down on her bed, the head rush took her too suddenly.

That frustrated Demetria more. She hoisted Rosalyn up by the arm and pulled her along, "You're getting dressed in my room. No sneaking naps! I have pants and a shirt you can fit. Good thing your coat is already downstairs."

The morning was another blur to Rosalyn. Before she knew it, she was sitting in the passenger seat of her mother's cherry red SUV in the family driveway.

The seat heaters blared at the hottest setting. Demetria stared at the road with an annoyed glare as she yanked the transmission knob into drive. The driveway was a little icy but Demetria didn't care, they were going to make their eleven o'clock appointment either by hook or by crook.

Demetria peeled out into the snow cleared road and zipped as fast as she could without the speed cameras clocking her. The ice-covered trees whizzed past as Demetria asked, "Where'd the new necklace come from? It's pretty." She had noticed it when she threw her sleepy, fussy daughter out of her nightgown and shoved a periwinkle turtleneck over her head.

Rosalyn wasn't sure how to answer. "Uhhh, well … thanks. I … got it as a gift from one of the booksellers downtown. The nice lady, Ms. Afuweti."

Demetria was touched, "Awwwww! That's so sweet! was it from a book promotion?" She was glad Ms. Afuweti was settling in well. The middle-aged bookseller had only been in the United States for a couple years and a New Tulsan resident for only the past six months of those two years. It wasn't easy to get a home here in New Tulsa as an outsider, international outsider or not. Distance didn't matter, anyone outside of New Tulsa was an outsider all the same.

"Yeah," Rosalyn lied. She didn't want to drag an innocent into her tale but she needed it to seem real. How else could she get such a pretty necklace? No job, no income. Online giveaways sounded too far-fetched. She hardly used her phone or the computer. It was just her and her books. "But she still has trouble talking so you don't have to thank her," Rosalyn shot her best sincere smile.

Demetria nodded, "Ah, ok. I hope those classes at BLM are doing her favors." Ms. Afuweti had a thick South Sudanese accent and English still tripped her up regularly. Definitely an outsider trait but not an abominable one. The classes were to simply boost her English, not eradicate her accent. To be the destroyer was certainly *not* the New Tulsa way.

"I think they are," commented Rosalyn. She certainly remembered hearing Ms. Afuweti have a bit of better diction as she explained to her employees where to shelve things when she, Rosalyn, was forced to volunteer a couple months ago. Ms. Afuweti was the only one there with an outstanding accent. Her teenage son, Ezekiel, had a slight accent to his words that only increased when he talked to his mom about something serious or frustrating. He was always nice to Rosalyn but not as charming as the Harlequ—

"As I hope that book club at BLM does *you* favors," mentioned Demetria with more than a hint of determination. "I'm not trying to push you hard, honey. But you have *got* to learn how to be social. College is more than just books. Especially if you go out of town. By the by, Medgar Evers University is always ready to take you in. Shanika works in Admissions and always asks me regularly about when she's going to see your packet cross her desk. And it isn't far, just a little past downtown on the west side. Really close to home."

Rosalyn sighed. She really didn't want to go to college. She didn't want a job. She didn't *want* to live in the scary, hyper-realistic world, full of bills, taxes, and drudgery. She simply wanted to be with her books. To be with the Harlequin.

A small, lovesick smile collected on her lips as she watched New Tulsa pass her by. As they left out of the sticks and neared the heartbeat of the town, there were more and more stores and sidewalks. Memorials dotted all over the town, dedicated to countless figures in Black American history, from statues to placards to vibrant murals. At the center of town stood an iron statue of an artistically recreated fire made with mirrors and broken glass donated from the families who survived the massacre.

They were encaptured by iron rebar ties wrought into a figure head outline of a person gazing out, traumatized. The mirrors and glass glistened as if the flames still lived deep inside their mind. At the bottom of the figure read a plaque encased in black cement:

There is no 'never forget'.
We cannot forget.
Only live.
For our children.
For our future.

It was named the Remembrance Memorial, the pinpoint epicenter of Freedom Square, right at the corner of Gurley St. and Greenwood Blvd. Freedom Square was where most of the town's festivals, celebrations and the occasional protest happened.

A couple blocks away from Freedom Square, Demetria parked in front of Deonah & Barb's Hair Salon. It was a bright, crisp sunny day with a clip of chill in the air. The sidewalks were salted as dripping clumps of grey snow hung about on the sides of the road. The clumps gave Demetria a challenge she didn't need as she parked, her nerves were already taxed enough. What a way to start March.

The shop had an old timey shop front from the 1920s, just like many stores in town did, but with a fresh coat of mint paint. Over the doorway waved the town's flag in the occasional cold gusts. It was stark white with a maroon Sankofa bird in the middle and a small, rising sun upon the bird's bended neck. The flag was new, the last one was burned earlier that year from some rednecks a couple towns over looking for trouble. They were quickly apprehended by New Tulsa police and still sat in a New Tulsa jail, their new home for the next decade (assuming good behavior). Hate crimes of any sort were *always* met with the harshest punishments in New Tulsa. The governor hated the heavy-handedness but no matter how many angry letters they got from people outside New Tulsa, they had to respect the historical "Savior Land" decree that was signed almost a century ago by a governor outraged by the original massacre. New Tulsa could basically operate almost like its own state … as long as they could afford it and didn't ask for help from the state.

Good thing the people of New Tulsa didn't simply find diamonds in their backyards. They already had their wealth and grand ideas. They just needed a place to flourish, unbothered.

The silver salon bell dinged overhead as Demetria and Rosalyn entered. The salon looked a bit old fashioned but still with the times. A big flatscreen sat on the waiting area wall at the front of the salon with the weather forecast going. (Prediction: another chilly week ahead.) Salon stations on the ground floor were filled with no-burn styling utensils and abundant hair cremes. A curved, iron-wrought staircase led to the second floor, where all the washing and coloring happened. Downstairs was the dry floor, upstairs was the wet floor, separated with lush, long rugs at the foot of the top and bottom stairs.

On the ground floor, Mrs. Barbra already had her chair ready for Rosalyn. They were a couple minutes early, thanks to Demetria's speeding and fussing at any traffic.

Women chattered away in the waiting area, seated in mauve chairs that lined the walls. Many of them were walk-ins or with late appointments.

Big in body, heart and spirit, Mrs. Barbra cheered as soon as she saw Demetria and Rosalyn, "Oh, here's my eleven o'clock! Hello, Demetria and little one!" She shuffled over to them as she marveled at Rosalyn, "Oh, look at you getting so tall! Demetria, she's gettin' tall like your mother! Do you feed her? Look at how skinny she is! My goodness, my goodness!" She barreled out a jubilant roar of laughter that shrank Rosalyn a little.

Demetria soaked up the warmth and passion. She smiled, "Awwww, you know all she does is eat books all day. I couldn't even get her to eat some ox-tail and rice the other day, so busy with her new book. And she *loves* that dish!" Demetria chuckled as she steered her daughter towards the prepared burgundy salon chair, "She has a to-read pile taller than her! Finally getting to it!"

From the washing station loft above, an older woman's voice astonished, "Is … is that *Rosemary?*" It was Mrs. Deonah, floored to see what the cat had finally brought in. "Little baby Rosemary? Oh," Mrs. Deonah hurried down the iron stairs, dressed in a beautician's smock with bits of water drips on it, "let me look at you, baby girl! You *are* getting' *tall!*" She clutched Rosalyn's arms and looked her over, even turned her around. She had on a dark brown coat, a ribbed periwinkle turtleneck, plain khaki pants and grey snow boots. A blue knitted cap with a speckled puff ball at the top was pulled down to her brows, her hair busted out wildly from underneath it. Mrs. Deonah continued to coo, "You're gonna be a heartbreaker one day! Demetria, you know it! Just gonna have scores of boys and girls falling at her feet! You seein' anyone yet, Rosemary?"

Demetria laughed uncomfortably, she could see Rosalyn already had crumpled into herself as she sat in the chair, she wasn't a fan of the fanfare. Demetria waved and shook her head, "Nah, no, Mrs. Deonah—"

"How could she not?" Mrs. Deonah remarked. She chuckled at Rosalyn, "You're not hiding them anywhere, are you?"

Mrs. Barbra interjected, "Dee-Dee, don't go having this child melting! Or it'll be another year before we see her again. Rosie, sit down in this here chair and I'll get started."

Mrs. Deonah couldn't help but to be mirthful. She still remembered when Demetria was brought in as a tiny tot and now, she brought in her own child. Granted, Rosalyn was the shyest person Mrs. Deonah had ever met but she still glowed with abundant joy at the sight of Rosalyn. Demetria's mother, Serena, still came in from time to time to get her grays taken care of and nails done. It was only once that she saw all three generations come in for a visit, back when Rosemary was a little girl, toting about children's library books. She always hoped to see that again one day. Instead, it was either Demetria by herself, Serena by herself, Serena and Demetria together or Demetria dragging Rosalyn in.

"Oh, alright, Barb," Mrs. Deonah took Demetria's hand, "We can go upstairs. Just a plain wash and twist for you?"

Demetria patted her flat braided hair, "Yup. And a trim for Rosalyn, maybe braid it."

Mrs. Barbra nodded as her wife led Demetria up the stairs. She knew Deonah would milk all the new life updates about Rosalyn out of her so she was sure she would learn everything new about Rosalyn eventually.

Rosalyn tried to stop her blushing from the previous interrogation as Mrs. Barbra inspected her hair. The salon was at a regular buzz as more and more women poured in for their appointments with the other beauticians. Rosalyn had forgotten her book in the morning rush, so all she did was try to focus on calming herself. She tried to use her phone as an e-reader, her last resort device. She never liked the feel of phone e-readers. Too wonky, too unnatural, too small.

Mrs. Barbra noticed something odd.

"Rosie baby? We might have to give you a full wash, detangle and comb. Ain't nothin' but twigs and leaves *deep* in your hair. Where on *earth* have you been? Runnin' through the forests in this cold?"

Rosalyn couldn't think of a good enough lie. Her mind was blank with the truth. The nightly visits, the kisses, the Harlequin—

"Rose? Are you listenin'?" Mrs. Barbra checked.

Rosalyn jostled out a quick, quiet answer as she twisted and stretched the ends of her sleeves, "The-the moon was so-so pretty. I - I wanted to see it - see it outside." She hoped that was good enough.

Mrs. Barbra knew of Rosalyn's moonlight sessions from Demetria, who would be baffled but then consoled that this was the worst she had to face, even in New Tulsa. And that mothers on the outside had it *far* worse. Mrs. Barbra herself heard it regularly from distant relatives and the internet gave no end of new horrifying tragedies to show for likes and clicks. Demetria was lucky. They all were.

"Baby," started Mrs. Barbra, gentle and kind, "I know you love your nature but wear a hat or something, honey. You have *so* much hair to clean. Protect it, baby girl. You want me to braid it after I trim it?"

"No, no!" Rosalyn perked. Mrs. Barbra jumped a bit from the reaction. Rosalyn lightly patted her hair and continued in her usual quiet, "Keep it like this."

Mrs. Barbra obliged with a resigned huff, "Allllright, but promise me you'll work harder to keep it clean."

"Okay," Rosalyn agreed.

The remainder of the salon visit was pretty plain — except when Demetria got a bigger bill than she expected and the connected story. That was a matter of discussion in the car as they drove at a regular speed to the book club on the other side of downtown.

"Rosie, the bill came to forty-five dollars!" Demetria lamented as she kept her eyes on the road, hair clean and twisted down to her shoulders. The Sunday traffic was a bit choked but nothing infuriating. "Why'd you have half of the forest in your hair? I even saw the bits and bobs they got out! Have you been *sleeping* outside? In the *cold*? It's *snow* out there, how in the *world* did you manage all this? The bill could have been *seventy-five* if they didn't cut me a break!"

Rosalyn didn't really have an answer. "I'm sorry," she mumbled.

Demetria let out a haggard sigh, "Rosalyn, you gotta not *do* things like this — or at least plan to wear a hat! You're growin' up. Boys might find you a bit weird if you do things like this! Girls, too." Demetria had never seen her daughter show any affection or endearment towards anyone *not* connected to the fictional world but that didn't mean it would never happen. Even Devonté has occasionally shown an eye for something that *wasn't* video games from time to time. She and her husband just wanted their kids to be prepared. They themselves, too.

Rosalyn shrank in her seat, face hot. She would really rather be in the woods right now. Her hair was fresh, clean and tucked into a low bun, mother's orders. She hated dating talk. She felt she could go a million lives without ever discussing it.

"Rose," started Demetria, calmer. She had to remind herself to not push so hard on her youngest. This wasn't the outside world. "Rose, honey … I just want what is best for you," Demetria admitted. "I know I tell you lots but the world outside of here isn't like what you expect. Not everyone is like us, honey. Some people are so full of hurt, they can't *wait* to put that on others. I just don't want you hurt by them."

Rosalyn remained silent, as she stared out of the window.

"Babe, don't be in your own little world while I'm talking," Demetria sighed.

"I'm not," Rosalyn softly replied. She continued staring out the window as they drove on.

The BLM Community Centre was close. Wasn't hard to spot, massive adinkra flag banners ran down almost the entire length of the russet bricked building. A new addition to town in recent years, paid for by a New Tulsan tech maven, Benlie Thomas. She came back home when she saw the countless justice protests and riots that popped up all over the nation. None of the troubles struck New Tulsa — though it wasn't from a lack of earnest effort from the same people who destroyed Tulsa the first time. The maven merely wanted to let New Tulsa see the home support she knew they deserved. The opening ceremony was lovely, especially when Benlie declared when she cut the ribbon, "I know we don't need this. But I had to let my town know that I'm home in my own little special way. And that we'll never burn again. State of the art, best of the best. New Tulsa, welcome to the future."

It was also since the ribbon cutting that a new sprout of tech businesses and institutions sprang up around the community center. Benlie *really* wanted to show that she was home to stay. The sector was named Wonder City. The community center sat as the core of Wonder City, surrounded by arcades, including a couple mixed reality arcades. There were institutes for STEM of all ages, production centers of technology, comfortable factories filled with towering benefits, libraries equipped with imaginariums, the lot.

There also would have been far more neon and bright lights in Wonder City if the mayor, Aliyah Winters, didn't step in with a reminder to Benlie that not everyone wanted to live in a strobe light show. Benlie gifted City Hall with a glowing statue deposited squarely on the lawn as a reply.

The statue was of a little Black girl and a little Black boy both reaching for shining diamond stars, all made of wires and lights. Every winter, hand knitted scarves graced the necks of the statue children. Sometimes, even cute, knitted hats. This year, both scarves were plush and royal blue, visibly crafted from artisan yarn. No one knew who made the scarves but no one cared to find out, everyone thought it was a nice touch. The local museum collected them to have on display and for preservation.

It took a bit of waiting in some surprise downtown traffic but Demetria and Rosalyn finally arrived. They parked in the diminutive, half-filled parking lot of the BLM Community Centre.

Demetria and Rosalyn hopped out the car. Demetria looked pressed and Rosalyn looked as if she was getting marched to her execution. Wonder City was way too vibrant and social for her. Devonté loved it here, though. And Wonder City loved him back, several institutes vied for him due to his grades and loved his adoration for gaming technology. Benlie just wanted him for the e-sports team she wanted to form, the Talented Tenth. Devonté always turned down Benlie's offers, though. He just liked winning tournaments for himself. However, that didn't mean Benlie would stop trying, although. The desk he played on was a gift from her a couple tournaments ago. She wanted him to be one of her Cherished Ones. Anyone who caught her eye somehow, no matter how, could become one.

But today on this chilly day that seemed to become chillier, Demetria took Rosalyn by the hand and bounded up the short stack of long stairs. During the day, the stairs were a plain, dingy white, textured flight of stairs. But at night, the stairs glowed a brilliant white. During June, the stairs would circulate through all the pride flag colors. It was a regular photography spot.

Today, it was off and chunks of snow nestled in the crevices of the stairs. Demetria walked her daughter through the tall glass sliding doors, which bore a simple, eggshell white Sankofa crest and "BLM Community Centre" underneath. The cavernous grand lobby wrapped Demetria and Rosalyn with reviving warmth. Framed art from countless local artists around town lined the wooden, neo-modernist walls. The elevators had painted characters from games and Black culture. There even was a yellow Chocobo in the pose of the Sankofa bird at the information desk. Instead of holding an egg in its mouth, the green spotted egg was balanced on the top of its head, cradled in a small, brown nest. That also was the logo for the gaming and anime club there. The book club had a logo of a Sankofa bird with round glasses balanced on its beak and a book opened in front of it.

That logo beamed brightly on the televisions above the information desk, under the "Starting Now" list. According to the list, also starting now included a knitting club, an elder relaxation session and a resume crafting workshop. There even was a Shared Space Center, started by indigenous memebers of the city years ago but added to BLM Community Centre when it opened. They were intricately woven into New Tulsa under combined ownership of the city's land, something that was made official into the tenth year of New Tulsa's existence. The only reservations around were the many slots that filled the sign-in sheet on the door for pow wow gatherings, cooking courses, and children storytime groups. Winston used to take Rosalyn and Devonté to the storytime groups when they were tots. Actually, that was where his youngest found her love for books.

Demetria scanned which floor they needed to be on from the TVs. Second floor, left wing. Rosalyn was a pouting lump of weight Demetria whisked away into the elevators. The book club was set to start in fifteen minutes but Demetria wanted Rosalyn to do some mixing and mingling before she would become shut up inside herself like a telescope for the rest of the book meeting. That was Rosalyn for you, a total pro at mentally checking out at the slightest opportunity when in social situations — except when she was forced to interact.

The elevators dinged open and out Demetria lugged Rosalyn into the hallway of the left wing. The second floor was just like the first, filled with art and technology among the classic wooden decor. Demetria dragged Rosalyn down the hall as she checked every door until she found the correct room. She didn't want to pull on Rosalyn like a child, but it was either this or deal with her daughter's slow grave walking.

The silver double doors opened up to reveal a small library loft with a curved balcony and plenty of daylight from the long strip of windows that lined the front of the building from top to bottom. Metal, chocolate hued stacks lined up neat in marked sections. A carpeted clearing filed with a ring of comfortable, raspberry-hued chairs sat on the balcony itself. Already several participants were there milling about, idly chatting and catching up.

Rosalyn tucked behind her mother. She had enough of people for one day. Her mother's freshly twisted hair smelled of wildberries.

Demetria fettered out a woeful sigh. She could feel her daughter hiding behind her.

"Rose, no one will hurt you here. It's a book club." Demetria turned around to face her daughter, who looked terrified. She grasped her daughter's arms as warmly as she could and tried to explain as gently as she could, "They all like books just as much as you do, honey. It's just one *time*. If you hate it, we don't have to come back. Okay?" Demetria stepped aside to present the crowd, "Now, go say hello. They're nice, I'm sure. I gotta go sign you in."

Demetria patted Rosalyn's arm and left her daughter to her own defenses as she went over to the blue-grey checkout desk. A young, skinny librarian who wore a brass metallic nametag that read "Tariq Jonson" manned the desk. He was a little short and wore grey spectacles. I-Ching element symbols lined the blade of his copper hand and led into his sleeve. His peach shirt was crisp, buttoned up and nicely paired with a grey fair isle vest. His twists were about ear length and shook with his every movement. He had the brightest smile when Demetria walked up.

"Hi! Welcome to the BLM library, are you here for the book club?" Tariq asked, incredibly chipper. He was on his third cup of coffee so he had plenty of energy to spare.

Demetria nodded and started to fill out the sheet on the cork clipboard in front of Tariq, "Yep, signing in for one, Rosalyn Davis. I'm her mother, Demetria Davis. I won't be at the book club but I'll definitely be around in the centre." She wrote down her daughter's info and added her info as well, "She's *really* shy so don't be afraid if she doesn't say anything or stutters a lot. It takes her a while to warm up to people but she's not rambunctious at *all*. If so, call me." Demetria shot a pleasant smile.

The librarian beamed back. Oh, how many times he had heard that one and the kid proved to be a real demon the second the parent left the room. However, he had seen Rosalyn a handful of times before though, she was definitely a wallflower. He wasn't even sure he had ever heard her talk above a whisper or without a single stutter before. If so, it was that rare. Usually with kids like that, the real task was to keep them from being eaten alive by the other, far more vivacious kids. At least he knew which corners she liked to haunt: the far-off distant corner by the fire doors and art encyclopedias. If not there, anywhere that a social recluse would like to tuck herself in a small library. The quieter and emptier the corner, the likelier.

Rosalyn tried to start her way towards the small club of kids her age. She didn't want to go but she also didn't see much of a choice. It was either socialize or be grilled by her mother on the way home. She looked over her shoulder; her mother was already gone. Probably in the café downstairs to decompress from the morning.

Rosalyn didn't have far to go before a couple girls spotted her. They were a duo of goth punks. One was heavyset with silver-blue cornrow afro puffs, her companion was a little lighter but not by much. Her hair was short cropped and lime-peach. The both of them had fairly dark complexions. They were the Thunder Twins. Massive e-sports gamers, incredible computer whizzes and big believers that anarchy counted as a good time. They were best friends and a couple of Benlie's "Cherished Ones". Hacked a couple electric cars in a neighboring town for a joyride in a rich district and that's what caught Benlie's attention and made her smitten. The duo had seen a couple horrid STEMbro memes mocking them and their town posted by a hackerspace in the neighboring town. They thought it would be a nice strike-back to take a couple cars from the parking lot during an active hackathon from the members who posted the memes and test how fast the cars could actually go. Two electric cars, one silver-black and the other storm-wash blue.

Pretty fast, they learned. One even was souped up under the hood.

No one got hurt, the twins abandoned the cars at donut shop and hacked them again to spirit off into the distance until the batteries ran dry. They already knew the offending members had self-driving electric cars, it was easy. The twins gave themselves up to the police peacefully, no arguing, all smiles.

The hackerspace was thrilled to hear the Thunder Twins got nabbed — until they read the update that appeared later in the evening that Benlie sprang the girls out and placed *her* lawyers on the case. Turns out, it was far cheaper for the hackerspace and police department to repair a pair of ran down electric cars than fight a surprise batch of corporate lawyers, so all the cases and charges were dropped.

And lo, from that day forward, the Thunder Twins became one of Benlie's Cherished Ones.

To soothe the parents of the Thunder Twins, who were petrified to hear of what had happened to their daughters,

Benlie hired the girls to work at her company, Bene Electrics. They hadn't struck eighteen yet so they had apprentice jobs but were still salaried.

And here they were, with Rosalyn the wallflower.

"Hey, Rosalyn!" the silver-blue haired one greeted. She liked Rosalyn, she just wished she could figure out the code to make her more social.

Riveted to the spot, Rosalyn stammered, "H-hi, Ripper and Banks." She was sure that the Thunder Twins were going to push and prod her to be as social as possible. They always did.

Ripper replied as she fluffed her afro-puffs, "Nice to *see* you here!" Her voice was kind and a bit pitched. "'Ey, Banks!" she called behind her.

Banks was already sauntering up in an easy stride, she had a bit of a comparatively deeper voice, "I see her, I see her. Sup, Rosalyn?"

Rosalyn shrank into herself as she gently greeted, "Hi." Her face was hot and she wanted to go home.

Ripper bubbled, "We're picking a new book today, aren't you excited?"

Banks added, "Some folks are thinking of graphic novels but the book that came out a couple months ago over the holidays with the Forest King is a good one. We spent a lot of time on the last book and that one was a lil' boring, it would be nice to clean our palettes with something that *won't* put me to sleep." She gave a small, slow chuckle.

Rosalyn perked up. She almost forgot the book existed since the day she met the Harlequin.

"Have you read it?" asked Banks.

Rosalyn nodded.

"How far?" asked Ripper.

"M-maybe a third?" It was a rough estimate. Rosalyn loved books but talking about them was another story.

"'Ey! It's the Danger girls!" a young boy cheered from the library doors. He was immediately shushed by everyone but Rosalyn in the room. He dampened his volume with a sheepish smile, "Ah, my bad, my bad." He had small tattoos dotted all over on his dark brown hands and his hair was a neat duo of tightly wrapped small buns with an undercut. He had on thick, worker denim pants and a skull motif sweater he had knitted himself. It was Roderick but he had rather be called "Jumper". His dad owned an automotive shop and Jumper himself also loved cars. He also liked things that went boom, he was a regular runner in protests as part of the antifa. Fascism, racism, whatever, if he can explode it, it's a good day for him.

Also, he was another one of Benlie's Cherished Ones. He landed on her radar after going with a local antifa crew from a nearby town to break up a White supremacy rally half a state over. They needed his expertise for the colorful, the loud and the dramatic. And that, he certainly provided far beyond expectations.

Somehow, among the flash bangs and fighting around a Confederate horse statue with a Confederate flag draped around the horse's neck, Jumper not only managed to switch out the stars and bars with a trans rights flag, he also detonated fireworks and homemade smoke bombs around the statue. He attached the Confederate flag to one of the bigger rocket fireworks he had and up it shot into the night skies. Down the flag came under the brilliant flower spread of lights in charred and flaming tatters flickering to the ground.

The smoke bombs and dazzling fireworks were a smart idea, he needed cover and time to pull out of his bookbag one of his aerial drones to lift him out. "The Suitcase", Jumper called it. The drone looked like a regular suitcase, until it opened from the bottom to reveal strong propellers and homebrewed technology inside. The handle was for carrying The Suitcase like normal but it also was the grip for flight when pulled through to the other side of The Suitcase hinge.

Jumper would have gotten far but a rubber bullet got him in the leg and he crash landed in the woods of a nearby sundown town. He was discovered in the early morning by local police. They exercised little restraint when they found him waking up among the wild bushes. One of the local hikers took a quick video of the capture and a snapshot of Jumper's face as he was dragged out the woods to a waiting police car. His bruised face made the evening news and the video was splattered all over social media. It was only minutes after the news was shown did Jumper discover he had a couple power lawyers on his case and his bail was posted. Benlie personally picked him up in her car. Jumper had never seen a car so sleek and futuristic in person before. It was a prototype electric car, Benlie's design. She wanted to test some ideas out and had the company and money to do it. Now she went nowhere without her darling supercar, the L. Latimer x9085. Low body, immaculate design, all around ingenuity.

In all fairness, Jumper had no idea that it was even Benlie's doing until the crimson-gold butterfly door swung upward and he saw her with a waiting smile.

During the drive to his house, she picked his brain about The Suitcase and any of his other inventions. The car drove itself as Benlie was turned around in her ornate, cream white driver seat, facing Jumper as if they sat in a space shuttle cabin pretending to be a nightclub booth. The floor was a screen that pulsed stardust visuals to softly-playing trance house music on the sides but also showed the surrounding map of New Tulsa in outlines of gold on black as well as the route it was taking in a glowing maroon line. Jumper was tongue-tied from his wonder, his nervousness, and his injuries but he explained what he could along the way.

At his house, Jumper's parents couldn't stop bawling when they saw his mottled face in their hands. Jumper's father couldn't thank Benlie enough as Benlie tried to console Jumper's mother, who couldn't stop screeching with tears every time she looked her child over. It was a good thing they were New Tulsans, Jumper didn't have to fear seeing a hospital bill, healthcare was free citywide for all residents, from mental to physical. New Tulsa had the lowest fatalities and longest lifespans in the state and nation, both for Black Americans and in general. Old age was probably the biggest killer for New Tulsans. Second biggest was living anywhere else.

The officers pictured in the beating were still fending off Benlie's lawyers to this very day. The lawyers were experts in dirt-digging and revealed the department had more than enough to cover up their graves.

Benlie told Jumper's parents that night, as they prepared to go to the hospital, that he either had to go under her wing or be hounded until he did. In her words: "I ain't losin' him to a bunch of pricks up in San Fran. They wouldn't even know what to *do* with him. I hate leaving money laying around for other people to stumble over." Jumper was already in trade school to be a mechanic but Benlie wanted him on her Innovation team, at least part time.

And lo, he thus became a Cherished One.

A very easily excited Cherished One. He zipped up to the Thunder Twins and Rosalyn. He had a bit of a limp but he got around fine.

"I heard y'all were here, I want to join and talk books," he joked. He was more of a fixture at the anime club downstairs. He would read a manga cover to cover but a regular book was no dice, too boring.

"Anime don't meet up until later this week," laughed Ripper. "You really here for the book club?"

Jumper snickered back, "I saw y'all in the window." He gestured towards the massive front windows. "I was across the street puttin' in hours at Ben Tech," it was his name for Bene Electric, Benlie's research and innovation facility. He noticed Rosalyn.

She was very shrunken into herself. Head down, hands clasped and arms folded to her chin.

Stunned, he apologized, "Oh, was y'all talkin'? Aww, I'm sorry!" He greeted warmly, "'Ey, my name's Roderick but everybody calls me Jumper. You are?"

Rosalyn tried to say her name but got stuck in a stammer instead. Embarrassment flared within her when Banks answered for her.

"This Rosalyn. Her brother's Devonte.Inferno, you 'on't remember him from last year's tournament?"

Jumper racked his brain. There were a lot of people at that tournament. Including his now ex-boyfriend. Good times then, miserable memories now.

Ripper filled him in, "The one who won grand champion?"

A light finally clicked in Jumper's head. "Ohhhhhhhh! That dude!" The more he remembered, the more he reveled in a growing smile, "Alright, alright."

Banks gestured at Rosalyn, "That's his sister. She's a lil' on the shy side but she's cool."

Seeing how sheepish Rosalyn was, Jumper muted his personality the best he could to help Rosalyn warm up a little faster. "Oh, well then. I shall leave you ladies to it," said he. He then gave a royal bow, "I bid you all adieu."

"You not stayin'?" Banks questioned with a snicker. She knew prose books were not his cup of tea. She gave him an audiobook once to listen to as he repaired the drivetrain under her car. Found him fast asleep with oil dripping on his forehead.

"Gotta put in more hours. Just wanted to stop by and say hello," he grinned. He waved goodbye and made his way to the doors.

Tariq stopped Jumper as the Cherished One passed his desk, "You're not staying?"

"Nah, I'm good," replied Jumper and out he left.

Tariq sighed and left from behind his desk. "Everyone," he announced, "let's get ready for book club. Can we all sit in the ring of chairs? Thank you."

Everyone's milling and chatting drifted over to the ring of plush chairs as they picked their seats. Rosalyn wasn't the only newcomer, new members were only added when a new book was being picked, so to not disrupt the flow. Rosalyn picked the chair near the librarian and the Thunder Twins sat beside her. The circle was full of all sorts of people, young and old, clean-cut to punk.

The librarian clapped his hands softly and announced, "So many new faces! I hope you all stay. I'm Mr. Tariq Jonson, I'm the librarian here at BLM library and this is the BLM Community Centre's book club. We have some ground rules before we begin…."

Rosalyn was already mentally checked out. She thought about her morning, about her evening. How the Harlequin accepted her name for him. How he would leave her phantom kisses and where they were left. How he adored her. How she adored him. How much she wanted to see him again—

A light clap from Tariq jostled Rosalyn back to reality.

"Okay, everyone! That concludes our book club for today. There are copies available but we can get more if needed. Thank you all for coming!" Tariq got up from his seat and started to head back to his desk, where Demetria already stood waiting with clasped hands and a hopeful smile.

"Rosalyn," Demetria called gently. Everyone milled past her, including the Thunder Twins, who waved goodbye to Rosalyn.

As Rosalyn got up, she wondered how much time had passed. It certainly didn't feel that long. She shuffled to her mother, who asked with a hopeful lit, "Did you like book club?"

Rosalyn shrank into herself as they both walked down the hall together.

"It was fine," she reported barely above a whisper.

Sounded promising to Demetria. Now, for the billion-dollar question: "Do you want to come back?"

Rosalyn took a bit of time to answer. "… No."

Demetria dropped her head, defeated and resigned to accept her daughter's answer. "Fine. Fine. Thank you for at least trying."

Chapter 4

The drive home from the BLM Community Centre was quiet. Rosalyn dropped out of any and all social engagements she wasn't forced into. She didn't do cookouts, parades, get-togethers, nothing. If she was pushed hard enough, a teary meltdown was sure to follow. Demetria and Winston simply wanted to figure out how to get their daughter past this before college. She had always been this way, ever since she was little. Even in pre-school, Rosalyn hid from the other school children and had meltdowns if she was forced to play with others. Devonté was more of the social butterfly, even as a tyke. The parents were at least grateful that Rosalyn didn't have meltdowns when she played with her brother, even as a child, but it wasn't long before the siblings' interests differed too much. But they would at least still play in the river in the woods together during the summertime. That was perhaps the only place Rosalyn's family saw her so happy and lively around others when not nose-down in a book.

Finally arriving at home, Rosalyn went immediately to her room. The day exhausted her, she needed a nap. She changed into her nightgown and dug herself deep under the covers.

Drifting off was easy. What she didn't expect was to be in the woods behind her home, floating above a loose bed of brambles, snow and leaves. Leaned over her was the Harlequin kissing her awake under the dappled afternoon sunlight.

Rosalyn was stunned. She tried to shift her legs but the brambles, snow and leaves simply pushed out of the way. Panic ebbed away from Rosalyn when she noticed the taste of pine and sweets. It was her Harlequin.

She accepted the kiss, even placed a hand on his head. The diamond pattern of his cowl was textured with the finest spun cord she had ever felt. It was unlike anything she had ever touched. The diamonds were smooth, the horns firm to the touch.

The Harlequin broke the kiss. He gazed upon her with a desirous smile and a little laugh.

"My apologies, Midnight Maiden," he said. "I couldn't help myself. You starved me with your absence, I can't help but hunger for you."

Rosalyn smiled back at him. She couldn't be more charmed.

The Harlequin stood back with his arms out. The brambles, snow and leaves flittered back to the ground as Rosalyn was lifted upright and set down in the snow. She had on no slippers but the snow didn't bother her at all. She could certainly feel the snow but not the cold it should have brought.

Rosalyn approached the Harlequin and hugged him. Head laid against his chest, she couldn't hear a heartbeat but she didn't care. Perhaps it was elsewhere. Maybe it was her pendant. She was just glad to be in his arms.

"Beautiful Midnight Maiden, it's still daylight," mentioned the Harlequin. "Let me find you a place to rest so you may be most splendid in the twilight."

Before Rosalyn could answer, they both heard Devonté call her name from the back door. He had on a winter coat, black duck boots and his navy plaid pajama pants. He left from the white storm door and walked towards the woods. Their mother had told him to gather her for dinner and that if she wasn't in her room, she was probably out exploring the woods. And to make sure she had on a hat if so.

Rosalyn grew panicked. She had no idea how to explain the Harlequin, nor did she want the Harlequin to abandon her because someone from the real world paid a visit.

She patted the Harlequin on his chest as she pled, "Harley, Harley, *please.*"

The Harlequin was unmoved. He held Rosalyn in his arms and kept a steady stare on the meddler sauntering to the lip of the woods calling their name for the Midnight Maiden, his maiden.

"Rosa-*lyn!*" called Devonté. The day was a bit warmer than last week but it was still cold outside. He wanted to find her quickly, collect his dinner of turkey and carrots, and head up to his room to prep for a raid later in the evening. His phone had already been buzzing about it all day. He also wanted to catch up with the Thunder Twins since they told him they spotted his sister and spent book club with her. She seemed mentally absent, off in her own little world, they said. Far deeper than usual, at that. Devonté wanted more details. He wanted to make sure his little sister was treated right by his friends and gaming buddies when he wasn't around. He also wanted to hear more about her spacing. He was glad *someone* noticed. He trusted the twins, they were fond of Rosalyn.

Devonté entered the brambles and stepped among the trees. The woods were crowded, snowy and bare. Wherever Rosalyn was, she must have been far. He couldn't see a single soul.

"Rosalyn, it's time for dinner, sis!" he called into the woods.

Still nothing.

Devonté was thankful for the many years he played in the woods growing up. Otherwise, the layout would have terrified him. He knew there was the river far ahead. He guessed his sister would be there, most likely lost in yet another book fantasy. As far as Devonté was concerned, nature was where his little sister was the liveliest. "Rosa-*lyn!*"

Rosalyn and the Harlequin watched the brother come closer. He was only mere yards away. They could clearly hear him calling her.

Rosalyn wanted to yell for her brother to go away, to be left alone. She patted the Harlequin's chest again, "Harley, he - he won't under*stand*. He won't understand." Her face grew hot. Tears were coming, she could feel them. She hid her face against the Harlequin's chest, "He won't under*stand* us."

The Harlequin's mouth gathered into a hateful sneer. "What a meddlesome sire. Ruthless." The Harlequin extended out an arm towards Devonté. "He praises the light for only himself and brings terror to the dark. How dare he? You are my prize and my gift alone."

A thorn bush caught Devonté's pajama pants leg. It surprised him, he was sure he was vigilant for all nasty brambles. But apparently, he missed one. A new one he had never noticed before.

Rosalyn watched her brother unfix himself from the thorn bush that quickly latched on from behind a tree, woodsy prickles tangled into his pants leg. She traced the Harlequin's outstretched claws to his hateful sneer. Alarm flooded her.

"Harley," she begged, "don't hurt him! He means no *harm*. He just won't understand us!"

The Harlequin's sneer dropped into surprise and he slowly looked at Rosalyn. Her face was teary and afraid.

"Do you wish me to spare him?" the Harlequin asked, floored.

Rosalyn nodded briskly. "He's harmless."

The Harlequin looked once more to Devonté. Devonté had finally managed to unlatch himself from the thorn bush and continued his way into the woods, calling for Rosalyn.

"You share your heart, Midnight Maiden," the Harlequin whispered, heartbroken. He traced a claw over her cheek.

Rosalyn buried her head against the Harlequin's chest but then he disappeared. All at once, the cold surrounding her bit into her. The chill brought her to her knees as she cried out for the Harlequin.

"Harlequin? *Harle-quin!*" The air she sucked in chilled her lungs so. Everything numbed her viciously as she shivered violently from the sudden, lancing cold.

Devonté's head snapped to her as soon as he heard her cry out. She was practically in front of him, only a few yards up. He couldn't believe he didn't see her before.

"Rose!" he dashed and skidded to her aid, his feet made a long wake in the snow as he slid to her. She was rattling, barefoot … and there was a weeping cut on her cheek. He ripped off his coat and threw it upon her. "What are you *doing* out here without a coat on? Where are your *shoes?*"

Rosalyn bawled terribly. She wanted to call the Harlequin back but she was too cold and choked up to form sensible words. She dropped her head and pulled the puffy down coat tighter around her. Devonté tried to help her to her feet but the searing, ferocious pain made her sink back down to her knees. A drip of blood pattered onto the snow, but she didn't notice from her vision blurring from the tears and cold.

Questions would just have to wait.

Devonté gathered up his sister and picked her up. He was glad she was fairly light and he took a weightlifting class last semester. He saw what a mess she was; there was no way their parents wouldn't grill them. He would miss his raid for sure. But why was she outside in the freezing cold? *None of her book crushes made her act like this before*, he wondered.

Meanwhile, both parents were in the basement. They were studying the hot water boiler for frozen pipes. When

Demetria tried to wash her hands for dinner as she told her son to gather his sister, she found the kitchen sink leaky at best under full blast. Devonté watched his parents go down the basement stairs as he got on his coat & boots. Now, with his little sister in hand, he could see the basement light bask through the small white paneled window in the house's concrete foundation.

This gave Devonté an idea.

"Okay," he started to explain over Rosalyn's tears, "what we're gonna do is stay as quiet as possible. Ma and Dad ain't got to know but we *do* need to *talk*. Got it?"

Rosalyn sniffed and nodded. She tried to stifle her tears and whimpers as much as she could as Devonté carried her into the house. The thorn bushes didn't give him any bother on the way back, except for a couple small snags here and there. Snow crunched under his feet in speedy rhythm as he rushed out of the woods, afraid his parents would discover them.

He struggled to get open the storm door and back door with Rosalyn in his arms but he soon managed. In a flash, he hurried her into the house, up the stairs and into her room. His boots clomped but he hoped his parents wouldn't care as they continued to busy themselves with the boiler.

Devonté dumped his little sister on her bed and closed her door. He had a bit of a shiver himself from the cold, his plaid pajama top was no match for the bristling cold outside and the deep chill ate at his bones. He barely could feel his fingers, much less his hands.

As the warmth started to melt the cold within Rosalyn and return sensation to her body, Devonté asked with a muted temper, "What on *earth* had you goin' *out there?* It's literally *freezin'* cold!" He was thoroughly beside himself, he struggled to keep his voice down. "Where are your *slippers?* Why were you *barefoot?* What is going *on*, Rose?"

Rosalyn bundled herself up in her comforters, dejected and embarrassed. She noticed her cheek stung. A small dab showed her a smear of blood on her fingertips. She didn't know what to make of it.

"And you're *hurt*, too!" Devonté lambasted. He wanted to scream but he knew that would get him nowhere fruitful. Plus, he didn't want the parents to get involved.

Rosalyn looked up at Devonté, hopeless. Then her face crumpled as she whined out a small cry.

Frustrated but caring, Devonté tried to explain, "I'm sorry I got mad. But you literally were outside in just your nightgown yelling for a book character. I'll always let you do you but you can't be doin' *that*. What if I didn't find you in time? Then what?" Devonté wrapped his sister in a tight bear hug, "I love you, okay? You're my baby sis, the only one I got. It's on me to look after you." He pecked her on her uncut cheek and snuggled her. "I know you love your fantasy but you gotta be a lil' realistic sometimes, that's all."

Rosalyn whimpered out some more. The Harlequin abandoned her. She clambered for her necklace under her comforters. It was still there but how did she know if that meant he would come back? Or that it would soon disappear? The terrible sneer and his last words said it all.

You share your heart, Midnight Maiden.

Rosalyn blubbered out harder.

Devonté felt bad for his sister. He laid her down in her bed, adjusted the comforters on her and looked around her room for a box of tissues. He found a small, ruby box on her dresser, almost obscured by books. With a few snatches, he had a decent handful of soft tissues and knelt down to aid her cheek.

"The cut doesn't look bad," Devonté reported as he held the tissues firm against her cheek. He counted to ten mentally. He figured all it needed was air. Devonté bundled up the tissues in a ball as he consoled her, "You're gonna be fine. Stay up here, I'll get you your plate. If Ma and Dad asks, I'll say you were out in the woods but you had your coat on and everything. Just get some sleep, okay?"

Rosalyn nodded, teary-eyed and tuckered out.

Devonté rushed out her room and down the stairs to make her plate, his booted footsteps thundered into the kitchen. He screamed loud enough for his parents to hear him in the basement, "Rose is in! I got her plate! Gonna raid! Love you!"

He plucked out two coral orange plates from the cabinet above the double sink. He saw nothing but near darkness outside the kitchen window over the sink. He couldn't believe Rosalyn was out there in all of that as he placed the plates atop the silver stove and opened the oven door.

The oven light popped on and revealed a crumpled cradle of aluminum foil. Inside the cradle laid spice-marinated slices of turkey and carrots. A wooden handled ladle stuck out the top of the aluminum cradle.

Devonté took each plate and slopped on a couple thick slices of turkey and a decent bundle of carrots.

He thumped the oven door shut and plucked out a pair of recently washed forks and knives from the metal drying rack to the right of the sink. Plates made, Devonté darted back up the stairs with a plate in each hand.

When he entered Rosalyn's room, he found her already out, dead asleep. Her cut beaded blood but none spilt.

Devonté couldn't help but pity her as he looked upon her.

All this from a book, *wow,* he thought as he sat her plate atop a short stack of thick books by the iron leg of her bed near her head. He made sure to balance the knife and fork well. Last he wanted was for her to wake up to a soppy mess, and on her precious books, no less.

Satisfied with his balance act, he pecked his little sister on the temple and whispered, "Love you, gonna raid."

Devonté turned out the light in her room, looked back at her once more, and closed the door.

Time to raid.

Devonté slipped into his room and half-plunked his plate and silverware on his computer desk. He woke up his computer with a shake of his mouse. The computer blinked on, revealing a desktop a third filled with game icons. His wallpaper was of Storm summoning a tornado. He powered up his gaming dashboard by clicking on it in the toolbar at the bottom of his screen, where it laid minimized. His status pinged now as available, a green dot by his name as his gamertag, Devonte.Inferno, glowed cyan.

His room was tidy-ish by his parents' standards. All the clothes lived in a pile that slopped out of his closet. The carpet floor was clear enough to look decent, a recent feat after his mother blew her top about how trashed the room looked. All his bookcases were stuffed and overflowing, even the ones on his desk that surrounded his monitor cubby. His shelves were loaded with figurines from countless animes and games. Lanyards and plastic covered badges from conventions past draped down in clusters from haphazard spots all over. A few sports medals speckled among the badges, mainly for swimming, volleyball and track. The mangas were lined in neat order by series, he had full collections. His game cases laid about wherever they could fit on his shelves. Near his tall bookshelves, clumps of khaki comforters and white sheets laid strewn on his bed.

His second pride and joy, next to his Storm statue, was his gaming desk. A sickening rainbow of color beamed against the black pearl wash of the desk. Gifted by Benlie as a way to butter him up into joining her Talented Tenth but modified by him. A golden rack of headphone holders lined up the side, a translucent storm gray keyboard roll-out shelf with flecks of lightning strikes inside, a snack cubby, a squishy mousepad with a plump wrist bump covered in pink and gold graffiti with a sludge vomit style, and a drink holder, to name a few.

His entire gaming set up consisted of parts he received from gaming competitions and other parts he bought with his winnings. All of it was magnificent in all its beaming glory. Clear case tower, curved wide monitor, sideways gaming mouse, gleaming sleeping Lawson console, and a blue camo controller, which matched his gaming chair. The chair came along with the desk as part of Benlie's gift. It was to match his controller, which he brought to every tournament.

As Devonté checked his gaming updates, he saw a message from Bank$$$y.Thunder waiting for him on his console's friends list. The friend's name blinked in a gold bold font.

He opened the message as he waited to be pinged for raid. Today was gold digging day, Beepz already had a plan to get the most loot boxes from today's game, a stealth role-playing game called *Vicious Winds*. They had been working on picking this map clean for over a month. But that could wait.

Bank$$$y.Thunder: Ey, mang Checkin in wit chu over Ros. She was just in anudda *world* bro. Every time someone talked to her, she just ain' hear em. Jus letting you know, man She lost af in her head. The librain said to leave her alone but yeah, lettin you know

That wasn't good.
Devonté typed:

Devonte.Inferno: Thanks, Banks

He hoped this didn't get worse as he cleared his desktop to click on *Vicious Winds'* icon, a violent tornado with a stark black V outline. He waited for the game to load. Beepz hadn't pinged him yet but he wanted to do a quick solo session to clear his head.

Chapter 5

Two weeks and no Harlequin. Her brother kept a closer eye on Rosalyn now since the last incident. If she wasn't in the house, he went directly into the woods, where he would find her searching in her slippers and nightgown. These discoveries waned fast over the two weeks but he still grew concerned about her mental state. He even paid a visit to his school's counselor office to get a professional opinion of what his sister could be going through. He learned a litany of new smart-people words but none of the dense jargon seemed to perfectly match his sister. Every time he pointed that out, every professional he stood in front of would deliver their expert good-bye line: "Can't really say for sure unless I see her personally."

That wasn't happening. Rosalyn would probably have a monumental meltdown if he even broached the idea to her. She already would shut down around him and the family when her flights of fancy were brought up as a subject. She told him she was feeling better but he still had the nagging feeling something didn't add up.

The parents were a little less perceptive. Working to keep a home and family afloat can be taxing. Especially with a busted water heater on top. Both parents took on extra hours since they discovered the broken plumbing. Turns out, the pipes were indeed frozen and after some surveying taps, a couple busted wildly. They were lucky it wasn't the boiler. Turns out, according to the plumber, it tried to burst as well but enough water released that it didn't. Now, neither parent would step into the house until after six-thirty.

Though it had seemed like Rosalyn had calmed down in the eyes of her brother over those two weeks, she merely moved her searching to the daytime, when the house was empty because of school and work. By the time her family came home, she was bundled up in bed, softly snoring under the covers. Or bundled up, softly mourning under the covers.

Every day, as soon as the last house member would click the front cedarwood door shut, Rosalyn would spring from her bed, slide on some slippers and leave for the woods. She didn't want to change from her nightgown and slippers. Her hair was pulled back into a low puff-ball. She felt like a princess looking for her lost prince like this. She didn't want to believe that she was abandoned. There were no more phantom kisses but she still had the necklace.

The weather warmed up considerably over those two weeks, spring was trying to arrive and fast. All the snow had melted away and the days were moreso cool than nipping cold.

Rosalyn was thankful, she could search for the Harlequin for longer. Her searches were the only things that kept the depression from getting too crushing. She would travel to the river, she would even try to travel beyond it. The river was a line defined by the parents since she was little, all beyond the river was forbidden as it was untraveled and thus assumed dangerous for the children.

However, no matter how hard she tried, the first few rocks would prove too much for her. She had never tried to cross them before, only played on them in summers' past with her brother and parents. Dejected, defeated and dismayed, Rosalyn would slump herself back inside to throw herself into bed and go down another enhanced depressive stupor.

Today was another day of an empty house. Devonté was at school, Demetria and Winston were at work. Rosalyn headed out into the woods once more. She knew the hours to search and could tell when her time grew short by the shadows of the surrounding trees.

Foliage began to bud, and stalks of greenery started to poke through the groundcover in healthy sprouts. The birds started to return and a bit more wildlife scurried about. It wasn't the beautiful, ethereal snow but Rosalyn welcomed it all the same.

Rosalyn padded through the forest like she always did, slow and cautious. Hand on her necklace, she swept her eyes far and wide. She didn't want to miss a single sign of her lost beloved. Careful and cautious, just like she what she would read in her stories.

"Harlequin," she softly called out, just like she always did during these past two weeks. She wanted to be louder but worried someone unwanted would hear. The surrounding houses were spread relatively far apart in the woodsy part of town but they still were close enough to pry if they saw or heard something odd. Her neighbors were nice but Rosalyn didn't want to meet them here all the same. She didn't have a fitting explanation for herself. She barely had one for her brother, whom she told anything he wanted to hear to get him out of her business. She knew he meant well, but he simply wouldn't understand. No one would.

"Harlequin," Rosalyn called out again. Only the silence of the forest met her back. Just like the past two weeks.

He was gone. She knew it.

Ruptured by upset for being by her abandoned lonesome, Rosalyn broke into soppy, soggy tears. She had tried to keep the tears at bay for these past two weeks, or only to her pillow but she couldn't help herself this time. She didn't want to be discovered crying in the woods but the emptiness was crushing.

Head plunged in her hands, she sobbed, "Where are you, Harley? I'm so sorry. Plea-please come back."

Rosalyn couldn't help but let the levee of her emotions burst. She searched endlessly, day after day, night after night. Her nightgown's lace hem had small rips scattered about. She had to wash mud and dirt out of her slippers and gowns every time she came back in from her day searches before her family came home. She encountered nettles, thorn bushes, and the overall unpleasantness of searching in the cold over and over. She simply couldn't take it anymore.

Around her, a whisper. *Is it that you cry for me, precious Midnight Maiden?*

Rosalyn stood bolt upright and looked around.

Nothing but forest and foliage.

You search under the sun for me? Though you should be slumbering for the night?

"Har-Harlequin?" Rosalyn choked. She didn't know if she imagined things or not.

From nowhere, Rosalyn's smiling Harlequin stood before her, proud and charming. The wonder of his appearance astonished her briefly.

"Yes, my dear maiden?" he replied, his voice a near purr.

An almost insane smile crept onto Rosalyn's face. Her heart swelled, tears ran down. He was back. He returned. All her efforts were not for naught.

She wrapped her arms around his neck. He accepted her warmly, claws gently wrapped around her back.

"My Midnight Maiden searched for me. The night chases me again," said he, tender and reassured. "What honor, what joy ... I thought you had shared your heart and didn't want me anymore—"

"Never! *Never!*" Rosalyn choked. "I love you so much," she faded into a whisper, "I could never want you to leave. Not now, not - not *ever.*" She kissed him on the cheek. His skin was warm and soft. She broke down more. "Please never leave me like that again," she begged sobbingly. "Please - please don't abandon me like that ever again. I need you more than you could ever - ever know."

The Harlequin smiled, his claws curved around her waist and her crown.

"Do you truly miss me, Midnight Maiden?" asked the Harlequin.

Rosalyn cried out, "Yes! Yes!" She couldn't keep the tears from pouring, her emotions flowed out like a rushing waterfall.

The Harlequin lightly chuckled under her sobbing. He then asked, "Will you share your heart with another?"

Rosalyn viciously shook her head, "No! Never! I love you and only you."

"But what about the Ruthless Sire?" The Harlequin's mouth turned into a hateful sneer.

"I love you more!" declared Rosalyn. Anything to keep the Harlequin from disappearing again. Anything. "I love you more," she repeated as a whisper.

The Harlequin snickered to himself and slid his claws from around her to grasp her arms. He gave her a good look-over: She was a soppy, desperate mess. Cheeks awash with her tears — the scar still present — nose wet, and her face twisted in a terrible, sniffling frown.

The Harlequin looked upon her adoringly. He passed a hand over her face, it became dry and the scar disappeared.

Rosalyn felt all the sadness leave her, sucked away. All that remained was a quiet joy and gratitude. The Harlequin smiled at her, she smiled back.

She laid her head onto his chest. He lifted her chin with his claw and gazed down upon her. Then, he kissed her. She wrapped her hands around his head and pressed into his kiss harder. She didn't want him to leave. Not ever again.

Deeper and deeper they kissed, it was as enchanting as she remembered. Oh, how she missed it.

The Harlequin broke away first, which lightly confused Rosalyn.

"Don't you need your rest, dear maiden?" inquired the Harlequin. "The sun is out. Find me again, Midnight Maiden."

Before Rosalyn could panic or protest, the Harlequin kissed her again and she fell into a woozy sleep.

"Rose. 'Ey, Rozay. Get up, dinner's downstairs." Devonté shook Rosalyn again. She had been a deeper sleeper recently, he noticed. Even more than before. He figured her book crush had probably hit a bump in the road somewhere — something that happened from time to time — but he still felt like something was off. She was thoroughly depressed, that was totally new. All the forest explorations still bugged him also. He hadn't caught her in the woods recently but he had a sneaking feeling of how she spent her days alone.

Rosalyn stirred in her bed, soggy-minded and hazy. There were countless phantom kisses on her neck and heart. The sadness ebbed back to her but the kisses made her smile.

She stretched and greeted her brother, "Food?"

Devonté smiled comfortingly, "Yup. Pizza. Dad already got the fries but there might be some wings he hasn't found." It had been almost half a month since he saw her smile. It reassured him. He also noticed something else.

"Hey ... your cheek's better. No scar. Are you learning how to put on mom's foundation?" he questioned. He reached to feel Rosalyn's cheek, she pushed away.

"Sort of," she mumbled. She touched her own cheek and then touched her necklace under the covers. It was still there. Another phantom kiss touched her heart. She began to blush and she rolled onto her stomach to hide it. "I'll be downstairs soon," she bumbled out. Her bedroom light was on, it was night. A couple more kisses graced the back of her neck and her left shoulder blade.

"Ok," agreed Devonté. "Be down soon."

Rosalyn nodded. Devonté left her room and closed the door.

Why do you talk to the Ruthless Sire? whispered around her. Phantom kisses landed on her lips. There then was a light but present bite on her lower lip, covered with more kisses.

Rosalyn flinched from the nip of pain.

Did something hurt?

Rosalyn shook her head. She ignored the dull throb of the nip as even more kisses covered it.

It only hurts if you don't trust me.

"I trust you," Rosalyn whispered. "Wholly and completely."

Good.

Rosalyn got up to change for dinner. She expected her nightgown to have its tatters but the entire garment was immaculate and perfect. She was astonished. But, most of all, she felt loved.

She picked out a navy turtleneck and a fuzzy pair of pants from her closet floor. She wondered if the Harlequin could see her undressing. A quick phantom kiss on the lower corner of her waist answered her question. She sprang with a surprised yelp and threw on her shirt faster.

She blushed deeply, especially as she rushed on her pants. She turned off the light as she pulled her pouf out from her turtleneck and said to her empty room, "See you tonight, Harley." She left her room and closed the door.

The smell of delivered food, greasy, spicy and alluring, filled downstairs. Rosalyn met with her family in the dining room. She usually preferred to be dressed for eating so not to soil her nightgown.

Winston cheered from his stool, "There's my baby girl! We couldn't get the toppings you like so it's just cheese and mushroom. There's some wings in that bag if you want any." Winston already was on his third slice. Work was killer today, there was no way he was cooking. Demetria couldn't agree more, too exhausted to even think of a menu.

Demetria worked on a tangy, spicy buffalo wing sopped with viciously red sauce as she remarked, "Rose came down with a smile. She must be reading something *good*." She laughed through her clenched teeth as she pried meat from the bone. "How's the e-reader treating you?"

Rosalyn answered with a bigger smile, "Great." She sorted through the paper bags until she found a closed, fragrant styrofoam container taped shut with reapplied masking tape.

Popping it open, she found a golden red bounty of sticky, spicy buffalo wings, steaming and wonderful. As she pulled the container towards herself, Devonté checked the time on his phone and hurried to fish out a wide slice of cheese pizza.

"I got raid soon. Love y'all!" Devonté declared as he tried to shove some of the slice into his mouth and threw up a deuce.

He dashed up the stairs, zoomed into his room, closed his door, and threw himself into his seat as he still worked on his pizza. He pulled open one of the drawers of his desk and lifted his gaming headset off its magnetic charger, his favorite pair. He pulled them on as the headphones gleamed to life. The words "Law of the Lawless" gleamed in a traveling arc of colorful light across the headband. It was Devonté's newest acquisition, paid for with tournament winnings. It was part of the Lawson console set so it matched seamlessly.

He powered up his gaming dashboard and reported as available. His gamertag glowed cyan with a green dot beside it and he didn't have to wait long this time for a ping of a voice call from a party of three.

He accepted the invite and greeted warmly, "Yo, yo, yo, I'm here. Put me in and let's get it." He turned on his controller as his friends' names lit up while they spoke.

"Bruh," said P0p.killa with a Chicago accent, "someone tried to snipe me earlier in Destructo: Global Encounter, man! I swear, people *crazy* out here. Just 'pop! pop! pop!' and all these holes around me!"

"Did you get him back?" asked Devonté. He saw a game request from Beepz for a space war game, *StarDart IV*, pop up on his screen.

"'Course I did," replied P0p.killa, mock insulted.

Beepz's Detroit accented voice overlapped P0p.killa's, "Hey, you get the request? Sorry for cutting you off, Pops."

"I'm in," Devonté confirmed. The star fight was already well under way. Devonté's character, a military soldier with a cartoonish, over-sized chicken head holding a futuristic rail gun, spawned in among friends. Surrounding him was a skimpy alien cheerleader with an absurd sonic cannon on her blue shoulder; a shinobi ninja crouched and ready with a laser katana; and a giant, towering, stuffed teddy bear with a flopped-out tongue, "u die nao" scribbled on its belly as it held a comparatively smaller gatling gun.

"Alright, let's get it!" commanded Devonté and off his team went, to scour the galactic landscape of moon rock and twinkling stars. He asked the cheerleader, "'Ey, Pops, did the drop change today?"

"Nah," P0p.killa replied. "We got lucky because there's gonna be an update tonight."

"Tonight?" Beepz, the teddy bear, asked. "When?"

"When we all gon' be sleep," said N0.nonsense, the ninja. He had a heavy Bronx accent. "Unless you gon' be in Tokyo, we'll be cool," he laughed. The rest of the guys laughed with him.

The night was the same as usual raids. They collected loot. They collected kills. They yelled and blared, entrenched in the game. A normal night. Since they knew an update was coming, they wanted to pick the land clean so they could scoop up whatever they could before something would be gone in the next update. The devs always liked keeping things interesting and the players on their toes.

As they searched a vast, lonely space swampland together, Beepz asked, "Hey, Devonté, your sister's still acting off?"

Devonté always vented his worries to them. These past couple of weeks had been focused on his sister.

"She's smilin' today," he reported back, a smile crept onto his face.

"That's good, that's good," commented N0.nonsense. "Don't want nothin' bad happenin' to her, man."

Devonté checked his door, it was still closed. He said a little lower, "She's just so wrapped up in her books, man. It's crazy. She just forever be livin' in her head."

"At least she isn't running the streets," P0p.killa pointed out.

Beepz guffawed, "First of all, there are no streets to *run* in Nu Tu, man. They live in, like, the holy land of the negroes!"

"'Ey, 'ey," Devonté warned. "My town ain't Pleasantville, we just look out different for ourselves here."

"Oh," said P0p.killa plainly, taken aback, "and Chicago's 'Chiraq' by choice?"

"I ain't mean it like that," lamented Devonté. Here it goes, the usual sticky wicket with outsiders.

"Okay, well how did you mean it?" asked P0p.killa. He wasn't mad … but he was getting there.

Before Devonté could reply, Beepz agitated, "Ohhhhh no, don't start, don't start—"

"I'm - I'm just sayin'!" P0p.killa sarcastically stumbled over his words. "If Mr. Nu Tu Brand New wanna say somethin'—"

"Pop," Devonté sighed, "you know I 'on't look down on nobody—"

"That's what y'all *think*," P0p.killa snipped.

"Sense, *please* talk to him," Beepz grumbled. If he wanted to hear arguments, he could always go downstairs where his parents regularly went at each other's throats. It could be bills, it could be accusations, it could be literally nothing. Anything and everything was fair game. Beepz wished he could find more than menial jobs so he could save up, move out and finally be on his own. College wasn't exactly cheap, either. He always tried to push the loans he knew he eventually would drown under when it came time to pay back out of his head. At least with gaming, he had some control over his life.

N0.nonsense tried to mediate, "Hey, hey, look. We all Black at the end of the day. I thought we agreed to squash this. We agreed, right?"

P0p.killa sucked his teeth. "Whatever, we did." He huffed, "*Sorry.*"

Devonté rubbed his face, "Pops, man, we're a team. Alright? I - I …. I mean that. I 'on't mean to ruffle your feathers, bruh. Are we cool?"

P0p.killa sucked his teeth and remained silent. He was thinking.

The silence remained for a few beats.

N0.nonsense offered, "C'mon, man, don't be like that—"

"We good," P0p.killa responded dryly.

"Alright," clapped Beepz, "let's see if we can find more chests out here."

Gaming would have taken up the rest of the night but N0.nonsense had to head to bed early for his morning shift at the supermarket tomorrow. It wasn't a dream job but it kept the lights on and the wi-fi paid. The rest decided this was a good enough point to call it a night.

Devonté checked the clock: 12:45AM. He stretched his arms and arched his back. He usually would dim his set-up to "Nightlight Mode", where everything turned into a calming, sleepy blue, turn off his lights and hop into bed but he had something extra to do before crawling under his sheets: check on his sister.

His lights off and his gaming desk in Nightlight Mode, Devonté put on his boots and left his room to open his sister's door a crack. He learned by now it was simply better to already have the boots on, in case he had to dart off rather than try to lace them up in a panicked state.

Peering in, he noticed the room was dark — and empty. Alarm flared within him as he tore down the stairs in the dark, sleeping house and rushed out into the woods.

"Rosalyn!" he called out as he dashed into the woods.

Deeper into the woods, closer to the river, Rosalyn sat in the Harlequin's arms and upon his knee. Her nightgown had white butterflies perched upon her shoulders and fluttering about her. The Harlequin showed her golden dust rabbits from his clicking claws poised before her. They hopped about, leaving trails of swirling dust in their wake. The area shone bright with burning gold stars overhead.

"Does this enchant you, Midnight Maiden?" inquired the Harlequin.

Overjoyed, Rosalyn clapped in delight, "Yes! Absolutely! Harlequin, you're *amazing!*" The delicate dust figures were breathtaking to her. She only dreamed of this from her books.

The Harlequin's smile then faded as he looked ahead.

Rosalyn noticed and her face fell to concern. "Harley? What's wrong?"

"He who terrors the night," the Harlequin sneered, focused on the dark forest ahead. He could see the bumbling figure, walking by the moonlight's cast. The Ruthless Sire.

Rosalyn looked in the direction of the Harlequin's stare. Her brother. He had come to collect her — and scare the Harlequin away again.

Devonté could hardly see anything in this forest, even the moon wasn't much his friend. He remembered all the ins and outs but he forgot to bring his phone for light. His phone laid on his bed. He wanted to turn back but he had to keep moving. He knew the river was close, he could hear the surging water yards before him. But no Rosalyn.

"Rosa-*lyn!*" Devonté called.

Rosalyn's heart quickened. She threw her arms around the Harlequin's neck and plead, "Please don't leave me this time! Not again." She could feel the tears coming. "Not again."

The brother approached the lip of the river, bathed by the golden light that cascaded over the clearing but he seemed completely unfazed. He looked around, mere feet away from his sister but still appeared to see nothing.

"Rosa-*lyn!*" yelled Devonté. To himself, he worried, "Oh my god, I can't find her." He yelled again, desperate, "Rosa-

lyn!" The world was so dark around him. Maybe she wasn't responding because she was …

Devonté sprinted out of the clearing and tried to navigate out of the woods as fast as he could. He needed his phone for its light — and hopefully that was all.

Rosalyn heard his panting and rushing footsteps grow further and further distant. She worried for her brother. He just wanted to make sure she was fine.

The Harlequin steered her face to his, he wasn't smiling. "Does your heart cry for him, dear maiden?" A claw under her chin started to prick. Rosalyn winced. He asked, "Does anything hurt?"

Rosalyn tried to tilt her head upwards out of his hand but he curled his other hand behind her head and steered it to his face.

"It hurts because you don't trust," he whispered. He kissed her once. Then he kissed her again, this time on the neck. She felt a small bite that also made her wince.

"Harley…" she quaked, unsure of what to say next. "I - I trust you. I trust you."

The Harlequin pulled away and looked at her. Her chin was fine but there was a small swelling prick of blood on her neck. He passed his hand over it, healing it whole as he asked, "How shall you prove it?"

She gave it some thought. Her head was too mixed up to think of anything. She asked back, "How should I prove it to you?"

A delicious, cruel smile curled onto the Harlequin's face.

Devonté returned with his cell phone alight and a first-aid box he rummaged from the kitchen. He hoped it would be enough as he made his way back into the woods. He threaded through the trees as fast as he could. The light helped immensely as he steered his way through.

"Hold out your arms," requested the Harlequin.

Rosalyn did as she was told. Anything to make the Harlequin not leave her again.

The Harlequin laid a hand on her palms and pushed up both of her sleeves, exposing her bare forearms. The butterflies were all gone.

"If you trust me, this shouldn't hurt at all." Two long claws per arm, the Harlequin drew down his hand, leaving a clean trail of weeping blood behind each claw. Slowly, slowly he trailed down her forearms to her palms.

The pain bit her so, Rosalyn couldn't help but let out a curdling scream that rang through the forest.

Devonté heard her scream and sprinted faster to the river. He dropped his phone when his hand clipped a branch but he didn't care. He found her, laid on the ground in the moonlight-streaked darkness and freshly bleeding. She was sobbing, her arms were bloody.

"Oh my god, oh my god," panted Devonté as he rushed to her side and snatched open the first-aid box. He took out some crumpled paper towels he stuffed inside and rubbed down her forearms. He could see the glistens of blood in the moonlight.

Rosalyn whimpered and choked, "Harley, please. I'm so *sorry*." She was in such a painful daze.

Devonté tried to calm her as he wasted no time to dress her wounds. "It's ok. It's ok. I'm here," He reassured her — but also himself. "Iiiiii'm here. Big bro is here. I got cha, I got cha." He tried to joke, "Big Devonté comin' through with a power-up." It was the best he could do to keep the anger and tears at bay. Whoever did this to her was going to pay and *dearly*.

He saw that the wounds weren't deep at all. He thanked his lucky stars. He took out a roll of gauze and wrapped it around her closest forearm, from wrist to elbow. He tore off the end, tucked it in and started on the second forearm. He had no clue if he was doing it right, he just copied what he saw in his games and hoped for the best.

"Did you get a good look at whoever did this? Anything?" Devonté questioned. He was glad they were New Tulsans, the penalties against sex violence were among the most vicious in the nation. Even the governor would get worried from time to time, the penalties were so stiff and steep. Once cost New Tulsa a stop on an R. Kelly tour but it all worked out when they got TLC instead. Winston always loved to recollect that memory, it was where he proposed to Demetria, in front of the tour bus.

Rosalyn simply threw her head to the side and cried harder.

Dread panged in Devonté's chest. He blurted out, "You-you don't have to think about that right now, ok?" He gathered everything in the first-aid box as he suggested, "Just think of your favorite character and don't worry about it, ok? I'mma carry you to the house, don't try to walk." He clicked the box shut and ran up to get his phone. The light danced about madly as he zipped back to his sister.

He laid his phone face down by his sister and scooped her up. It was work but Devonté managed to pick up his phone and first-aid box in each hand with his sister nestled safely in his arms. Together, they left the woods.

Rosalyn was a quiet simmer of tears by the time they reached the house. No lights on, Demetria and Winston were very deep sleepers. Devonté delivered Rosalyn to her bed and sat her down like a delicate crystal.

As he took off her slippers one by one, Devonté inquired, "Can you talk about what happened?" He picked up the slippers and sat them by the door, which he closed for privacy. He turned on the light and went back to her bed. Her face was sopping wet, her gown dirty and her forearms bandaged. Her body shook with every sob.

Devonté turned the light off on his phone and laid it on the bed. He knelt down and took her hands into his. She tried to pull them away but he grasped them again.

"You gotta tell me about whatever you remember. You didn't deserve this. Whatever you remember," Devonté urged.

"You ... you won't understand—"

"I might not but that doesn't make what happened to you *right*," Devonté pressed. "Just tell me the truth and I *promise* we'll make sense of it all *together*. I am in *your* corner and I will back you up *every* step of the way. Every step."

Rosalyn looked at him and began to cough.

Devonté shot to his feet, "I'll get you some water!" He hurried out her room to get a lime plastic cup from the kitchen. He filled it from the clear water pitcher in the fridge. The cup and the pitcher jittered as his hands shook, he was a wave of emotions. He knew the second he got a good enough description from his sister, he was going to find the guy first. Him and his Lil' Slugger bat he hadn't touched since his Harley Quinn cosplay from the summer. He had faith in the New Tulsa police — and *only* the New Tulsa police — but he wanted a personal moment with the perp first. A long one.

He sped back up the stairs to his sister's room.

There, he found Rosalyn limp in the arms of the Harlequin. He was deep in the middle of a long kiss with Rosalyn, whose lifeless, bandaged arms dangled.

Wound up, Devonté threw down the cup and charged in, "I am *beat-ting* your sorry—"

The first swing went through the Harlequin and Rosalyn. So did the second. Baffled, Devonté looked at his hands and up at the Harlequin, who broke his kiss to smile directly at Devonté.

"Find us, Ruthless Sire," directed the Harlequin before he disappeared with Rosalyn.

Lost, Devonté stood clueless. The best idea he could have darted him out of Rosalyn's room and into the woods.

There in the clearing, he found the back of the Harlequin facing him. The Harlequin's hands were clasped around Rosalyn's head in another kiss as she was upright. Her eyes were closed and she appeared limp and lifeless.

The Harlequin looked over his shoulders and smiled again. Then, in a blink, they were all back in her room. Rosalyn laid in her bed, slumbering. There were new weeping cuts on the backs of her hands. Devonté saw them as he stood in the doorway. The cup of water he threw down was upright and full, the carpet dry.

The Harlequin flashed a slow, toothy grin as he stood in front of Rosalyn's bed. He then chuckled and disappeared.

Devonté rushed to wake her. He hardly could believe what he saw. He also noticed her bandages were gone and so were all her cuts, even the ones on her hands.

Rosalyn stirred awake. She could feel a phantom prick behind her ear. It made her tick her head towards her brother and crumple her face.

"Talk to me, talk to me," Devonté hurried out as he patted her arms. "Are you alright?"

Rosalyn opened her eyes, staring at her brother. Tears dripped down as she whined out, "He … Harley said I … I didn't love him enough." She broke into a light sob.

Devonté was even more confused. "'Harley'? Was - was that 'Harley'?"

Rosalyn turned her head away and continued crying. "You won't understand," she softly cried to the wall. She then nodded. "He wouldn't hurt me if I—"

"Ok, stop. Stop," halted Devonté. Nothing made sense. "*That's* Harley? What is he? Some kind of spirit demon or something?"

Rosalyn barreled out more tears to her wall, "You won't under*stan*—"

"I'm *tryin'* to!" Devonté blustered. "Honestly, I *am*."

Rosalyn continued crying. She wrapped her arms around herself and curled up towards the wall. She wished for more phantom kisses but was greeted with nothingness.

Chapter 6

Over the next three weeks, Devonté existed in a bit of an auto-pilot daze himself. Classes passed like a blur, life passed like a blur. The only thing that didn't was his memories and thoughts about the Harlequin.

Every night, Devonté checked on Rosalyn. He never caught her in the forest again, she always laid in bed. Day and night, he always found her in bed. When she was up and about, she was a depressed ghost. He regularly had to press her to eat. Any questions about the Harlequin brought thundering tears, an uneasy silence or both. The internet was no help and he had no idea how to tell others what was happening, so he simply kept it to himself.

Rosalyn searched for the Harlequin when no one was home. She was afraid to look for the Harlequin at night, her brother checked on her too much. But day after day, she found nothing. No matter how much she called and wandered. The depression drained her.

In Rosalyn's eyes, Devonté pried too much. She didn't want to harbor resentment towards her brother for driving the Harlequin away yet again but she couldn't help it seep up time and time again. He would ask about the Harlequin but Rosalyn could tell he just wanted to have an Inquisition, not simply understand.

Devonté wished he could understand.

"'Ey, Devonté!" P0p.killa called in his headphones. "What is *with* you? 'Ey, pause, pause."

The starscape of *StarDart IV* popped up with a pulsing "Paused Game: Someone in your party paused the game. Press A to resume."

P0p.killa asked squarely, "Dev, you need to talk to us and *now*."

Beepz agreed, "Pops is right. You're *way* off your game."

N0.nonsense added, "Is anything goin' on? Don't keep it in, man."

P0p.killa noted, "You haven't been right for almost a *month*. That's not like you."

"Is it school?" N0.nonsense questioned.

"We'll listen, honest," assured Beepz. "Whatever it is, you seriously don't have to do it alone."

"We *will* drive down to Nu Tu, you know that, right?" pointed out N0.nonsense.

Devonté didn't know how to open up. The truth was far too bizarre. Instead, he remained quiet.

The silence remained for a few beats.

Breaking the silence, P0p.killa asked, "'Ey, Sense, you can scoop us all the snacks at your job, right?"

"Make sure to get a six pack of pop," requested Beepz.

"For the last time," said N0.nonsense, "it's 'soda', not 'pop'."

"And for the very *last* time, it's 'pop', not 'soda'," refuted Beepz, with vocal support from P0p.killa.

"My sister is messin' with some weird dude screwin' up her head," Devonté blurted, a bit quieter so no one could hear him through his closed door. He noticed the Harlequin never visited him — but that didn't mean he wasn't probably listening.

Everyone in the voice chat stopped.

After a couple beats of silence, Beepz said, "Alright, to get from Detroit to New York. P0p, come over and bring whatever you got to handle this joker—"

"Whoa, whoa," cautioned Devonté.

"Nah, it's good, bruh," assured P0p.killa. "I've driven to Beepz before, it ain't that bad. I got a new knife I've been meanin' to try out—"

"Pops, it ain't that simple!" Devonté urged.

"It is where I'm from," expressed P0p.killa plainly. "You can't let some fool mess with your sister like that. Some of these lil' boys gotta get put in line and know the *law*."

N0.nonsense wholeheartedly agreed. "Pops got a point. Can't let *no*body do your sister like that. Gotta bring 'em up like their daddies should've."

Devonté wished he could get through to them without spilling too much of the truth. "No... no... it really is more than that."

"What could it be?" Beepz questioned. "He dazzled her with money or somethin'?"

"She don't seem like the Gucci girlfriend type," rebutted N0.nonsense.

"Are you both *serious* right now?" asked P0p.killa.

"It's-it's ... he's ... he's got power, y'know?" Devonté tried to explain.

Beepz was unmoved. "So? Your town *literally* has Benlie—"

"It's just— my sis may try to protect him—"

"Take her out to her favorite bookstore and we'll handle the rest, don't even worry about it," P0p.killa assured darkly. "I once nailed the head of police with a rock before, I ain't afraid of no 'power'." Worst stint ever in jail in P0p.killa's life — as well as his only. The head of police was trying to direct the police to use rough force to quell "rioters" at a peaceful justice march, P0p.killa figured a rock to the head would deliver some sense. He was then bathed in tear gas and pepper spray. He didn't remember much after that but he was pretty sure it was painful, judging from how sore he was when he woke up in the lap of his unconscious older brother in the police wagon. His brother still got jumpy around sudden noises, even the crack of a soda can would make him yelp and duck.

"Dev, look," established Beepz, "there is *seriously* no way around this. Lil' man just needs a quick lesson, we'll make it easy. Sometimes that's all it takes."

N0.nonsense informed, "I got PTO, it's doable for me. Plus, I heard you all in Nu Tu got a crazy style funnel cake I need to try."

P0p.killa chimed in, "Ooh, I've *never* seen Wonder City! I wanna take a picture on the steps!"

Beepz bubbled, ecstatic , "Oh, that's *true*! They *do* have the crazy stairs! I wanna try the VR spot—"

"Guys, can I check on my sis real quick?" Devonté never felt so lost.

Everyone agreed warmly.

"Go do that, man," said Beepz.

"Absolutely!" said P0p.killa.

"We'll be here," said N0.nonsense.

Devonté pulled off his headphones and muted himself. It was almost one in the morning. He had classes in the afternoon so he didn't care. He just wanted to check on his sister.

He peeked into her room. She was fast asleep in bed.

Devonté returned to his room, closed the door and placed back on his headphones. His friends were still discussing road trip logistics.

He unmuted himself, "Guys, I know y'all wanna help and that's great. I just don't know what to do about her head."

P0p.killa sighed, "I get you. My moms had the same set up. Had a boyfriend that treated her bad and *everything*. I would always wonder why she allowed that. I was, like, ten."

Everyone fell to silence for a moment. Then N0.nonsense breathed, "Bro, I ... I never knew about that."

Beepz joined in, "Aw, that's ... that's ... I'm sorry your moms had to go through that, man. Is she ok?"

Devonté had never known that about P0p.killa. "Bro, that sounds rough. How'd it get handled?"

"She eventually threw him out," P0p.killa replied. It was still a little rough to talk about. "She had to come to that herself but all my aunts really helped her see who he really was and that she didn't need that mess."

"That's good," commended Beepz. He sometimes wished his folks would split up to make the yelling stop.

They already had a couple rounds earlier today. First it was about the remote, then it moved to who never did what and other related subjects. He couldn't take it.

"I agree, good on her," added N0.nonsense. "Dev, just be there for her and everything will be fine. We decided to give this sucka two weeks' notice for him to straighten out his act. Just in time for the Nu Tu Jubilee month celebrations so no one will really bother us."

Devonté almost forgot: New Tulsa had a month-long celebration that started from mid-May and stretched to Juneteenth. The celebration was to remember the past and celebrate the future. The apex of the month was the anniversary of the Tulsa massacre and the end would be a massive parade on Juneteenth, where countless drumlines across the nation would visit and perform. He didn't notice the small cherry pickers wagons around town affixing temporary electrical boxes and hanging wired decorations around Freedom Square when he would leave the BLM Community Centre. Too caught up in his thoughts.

"Oh, Freedom month *is* coming up," groaned Devonté as he smeared a hand over his face. "Please don't act—"

"We're not discussin' this," stated P0p.killa. "He on two weeks' notice. You can let him know or not but we comin'."

Chapter 7

Devonté woke up late next morning. He still had a couple hours before his lecture class at two. An hour and a half of brain-numbing literature history, nothing he couldn't handle. Usually, his biggest challenge in that class was to stay awake. A feat far easier said than done.

He saw Rosalyn peek in. It was so slight, he almost didn't notice. Her fluffy hair poking out was the biggest giveaway.

"You need me?" Devonté asked, sleep still soaked in his voice.

Rosalyn shrank back in surprise and then came into the room properly. She clasped her hands and folded in her arms close.

"I … I didn't know if you were still here or not," she softly said. She appeared nervous.

Devonté sat up and patted his bed. "C'mon, we gotta talk."

Rosalyn stepped back and shook her head. Quietly, she said, "Harley wouldn't like this."

Devonté cocked an eyebrow. "What?" he asked flatly.

"Please understand," Rosalyn requested, her voice small. A gentle quake of subtle fear hid underneath her tone. She didn't want any more nips or bites. She already woke up from one on the nape of her neck and a small cut on her shoulder that she had a brown bandage over.

Devonté sighed, flustered and annoyed. "Fine. How are you?"

"Good," Rosalyn answered.

"Any visits from...," Devonté gestured towards the woods.

Rosalyn shook her head no. She wanted nothing more than the love of her Harlequin to return.

Devonté's phone beeped a techno tune under his covers. He fished out his phone and checked it. It was an all-call from Jumper on the gamer friend list. It read:

Hawaii 5.0. Stay away from downtown

Devonté knew exactly what that meant: New Tulsa was getting a welcome wagon visit from the surrounding White supremacist groups. *Now* he could tell that Freedom month was around the corner: The racists begin to pop up like daisies.

Another ping from his phone rang out. It was a community alert from the New Tulsa police. Rosalyn's phone rang a short concerto distantly in her room with the same alert.

Devonté opened the alert and read out, "'Caution, possible W. Supremacy activity located near Freedom

Square. Please avoid the area. New Tulsa Police'." He sighed, "Yup, Freedom month has arrived."

Rosalyn eyes grew wide. What other cities faced regularly terrified her. The world was such a frightening place.

Devonté could see the horror marked on her face. "Don't worry, sis. This is New Tulsa. We couldn't be safer," he smiled. He wasn't far from wrong, his phone pinged a new notification from his friends list:

**Ripper.Thunder, Bank$$$y.Thunder,
JumperJumpShot streaming!**

He could already guess what it was, live broadcasts of his friends causing mayhem to the invaders. Classic. He snickered to himself.

When he looked up, Rosalyn was gone.

"Rozay?" Devonté called out.

Nothing.

Devonté sprang out of bed and looked out of his window. He also saw nothing there but he still went to put on his boots.

Rosalyn tore through the woods as fast as her legs could take her. "HARLEY!" She screeched out. *"Harlequin!"* She arrived to the river and yelled out, "Please, Harley, take me *away*! I want to go *away*! I need you *here*!"

"My, does the Midnight Maiden love to disturb her rest to seek me?" purred the Harlequin behind her.

She whirled around and threw her arms around his neck. Rosalyn desperately needed his love, his care. She was sure of it.

The Harlequin oozed with adoration, "Precious Midnight Maiden, how quickly you run to me from the Ruthless Sire who disturbs your slumber." The Harlequin smiled. He kissed Rosalyn, who grew woozy in his arms.

It was daytime, Devonté could race to the river at record speed. He dipped and dashed through the trees. But no matter where he looked, he saw nothing.

"Harlequin!" Devonté bellowed. "Harlequin! Bring back Rosalyn!" He pounded his chest, "Take *me*! I'll give you what*ever* you want! Right here, right *now*! Blood, a soul, doesn't matter, but give her *back*! Ain't nothin' she's got that I *don't*."

An eerie chuckle arose a couple yards away. The Harlequin stood behind a laid out, sleeping Rosalyn. She floated with loose groundcover hovering beneath her. He presented her like a magician.

"Oh, Ruthless Sire," the Harlequin snickered. "She has something. Something very *worthy* of my affection." The Harlequin's hand lightly traveled over Rosalyn's body, slowing to her hips.

Devonté snapped, "Don't you—"

The Harlequin jerked his hand back in jest. A cocky smile smeared out on his face, "Such a beautiful rose." Before Devonté could charge at him, the Harlequin held up a hand. "Be at ease, so foolish and quick. I haven't plucked her yet." He brimmed with a subtle laugh as Devonté found himself bolted to the spot, unable to move. The Harlequin snickered more as he relished, "I've only brushed the petals."

Devonté boiled with wicked anger.

As Devonté struggled to yank his feet free, the Harlequin continued, "I'm sure when she's ready, it'll have the sweetest taste—"

"Not gonna let you do that. Not now, not *ever*," seethed Devonté.

The Harlequin doled out an easy laugh. "He who terrors the night, how interesting of you. But now, she must rest. For it is the night she lives for, not the day. Let. Her. Be."

The Harlequin placed his arms under Rosalyn and she lowered onto them. The groundcover dropped away. Then the duo disappeared and Devonté could move again.

With no time to waste, he darted back to the house.

In her bed laid Rosalyn, fast asleep. Devonté immediately went to shake her. She whined as she shifted about under her covers. He knew he had school soon, it was on the northside of New Tulsa, away from the fracas downtown. Plus, the university shuttle system knew how to change routes in the case of emergencies, classes definitely were in session.

But he couldn't leave her here, just waiting in the arms of the Harlequin.

Devonté pulled off Rosalyn's covers and bundled her up into his arms. She whined and struggled sleepily against him. She felt so dazed and woozy but she knew in her sluggish head that she didn't want to be in her brother's arms.

"I'm *tired*," she complained. "Put me back—"

"You're sleepin' in my room," Devonté told her. "I can take an off day, my attendance is good enough." He swayed a bit from his sister's physical protests but he managed to get her out of her room and curve into his, where she protested the loudest.

"I can't!" She yelped. "He'll—"

"You are *not* going to him," ordered Devonté. "You are sleeping *here*. Right where I can see you." Devonté dumped her on his bed, agitated at everything, including his helplessness and hopelessness. "Sleep *here*."

Devonté went to his desk to put on his headphones and pick up his controller. "Ain't nobody gonna die if I skip," he grumbled to himself as he got his computer ready for a game. He didn't know if his sister would watch his screen or slumber instead but he decided to play a relaxing, bubbly game about collecting charms and embers. It had a guiding corgi that followed along to warn of dangers like bosses or falling walls.

Rosalyn burrowed herself deeper into his covers, she had never felt so tired before. She watched some of her brother's gameplay but she eventually drifted off.

The day spurred by as Devonté gamed. He would check over his shoulder every once in a while, to ensure Rosalyn was still there. There she laid, dead asleep. As he gamed, he couldn't help but think about his meeting with the Harlequin. How the Harlequin was so self-assured, so mirthful. So … creepy.

He couldn't let his crew meet this guy.

"Devonté?" Someone tapped him on the shoulder.

He jumped and pulled off his headphones. It was his mother, Demetria. He paused his game and checked behind himself. Rosalyn was there, sound asleep.

He then returned to his mother, "Yeah, Ma?"

"Dinner's downstairs. Your dad made roast," informed Demetria. She and her husband were finally free from their overtime stints to pay for the boiler. This called for a celebration, at least a nice dinner.

"Oh, cool," Devonté acknowledged. He ticked his head towards his bed, "I'll wake her. She felt like reading in here."

Demetria nodded and smiled. Sometimes Rosalyn would curl up wherever when she had a good book. It wasn't uncommon for Demetria and Winston to find her in their bed, curled up and reading. Sometimes napping with a book beside her.

"Alright," Demetria chuckled. "And don't forget to pack for this weekend. Your father and I think a small getaway to the sea is in order. Just a weekend trip."

Devonté brightened, he loved beach trips. "Aw, really? Where?"

"To Diamond Beach," Demetria answered. "We're gonna leave early in the morning so we can beat the traffic. Your dad and I rented a nice little Victorian beach house overlooking the beach and the sea."

Devonté brimmed with joy. Maybe a change of location could also help his sister, get her away from the woods.

"Just get ready for dinner, ok?" Demetria said as she patted her son's shoulder. She left out his room, leaving the door cracked.

Devonté got up and stretched. He walked to his bed and rocked Rosalyn. "Ey, we gotta get up. Food time."

Rosalyn stirred, still saddled with slumber. Dusk had already fallen but she was still dead tired. "Ten minutes," she said, muffled by the covers. "I'll join you, Dev."

He didn't want to leave his sister alone but he also had nothing in his stomach. Hunger had only just hit him. So did his bladder.

"Look, I'mma hit the bathroom real quick and we'll go down together." He pecked her on the cheek, her closed eyes winced. "I'll be right back."

He went down the hall to visit the bathroom and washed his face in half time. When he returned, Rosalyn was still in bed, back to sleep. Devonté checked the window. It was dark, only a few clouds strolled by. The moon hung crisp and clear. He looked back to his bed and she was still there.

Hunger truly gnawed at him but he didn't want to leave her alone.

Devonté left out of his room and trumped down the stairs. The roast was already sliced and ready on the table. His dad checked the greens burbling on the stove, his mother poured herself a glass of apricot juice at the dinner table.

Winston smiled, "Hey there, Mr. Game Boy—"

"Gotta raid!" interjected Devonté as he passed between the kitchen and the dining area like a whirlwind. He collected heaps of food on a single plate as he sped out, "Rose still sleep in my bed, I'll share with her. Thanks, Dad!" He dashed off as he yelled behind him, "I love you! Can't be late!"

Demetria and Winston stared at each other, floored.

Devonté sped up the stairs and back into his room. Rosalyn was still there. He closed his door, placed the plate and silverware down on his desk, slid on his headphones and continued gaming as he ate.

And like that, Rosalyn was gone.

Chapter 8

Deep in the woods, Rosalyn was awakened by the Harlequin's kiss. She was laid against him, propped up on his knee. Golden stars shone above for light.

The sudden embrace startled her but she accepted it once she tasted the pine and sweets. Before she could get too comfortable in his embrace, there was a nip on her cheek that made her break the kiss and stare at the Harlequin.

"Did something hurt, Midnight Maiden?" inquired the Harlequin with a wide smile.

Rosalyn pressed a fingertip to her searing cheek. She didn't want to check for blood, too scared to. She looked down.

"Does it hurt?" questioned the Harlequin. He tilted his head inquisitively, "Why does it hurt? If you loved me, it would feel as gentle and comforting as a breeze." Slowly turning to hatred, the Harlequin righted his head and continued, "This shows how little you trust me, how *little* you love me. Though I have adorned you with pretties and glory, Midnight Maiden." His voice dissolved to hurt, "Do you not love me?"

Rosalyn blurted, eyes hot with tears, "Of course I love you—"

"Then why does it hurt? Feel unpure? *Unloving?*" accused the Harlequin. He returned to hurt in his tone, "Why? Why, my precious and glorious? Do you share your heart? You love him as well, *don't you?*"

Rosalyn's jaw jabbered with speechlessness. She tried to find something to soothe her Harlequin. "He … he's my brother—"

"Fine," brushed off the Harlequin, done with her. He couldn't even bear to look at her as he waved her away. "Go. Go be with your one true love. He who is the terror of the night. The Ruthless Sire. Let him be enchanted by the stars in your hair like I once was."

Rosalyn's lip quivered, her heart torn to pieces, "Please—"

"No, I thought your heart was pure but now I see it's divided." The Harlequin's mouth was twisted with disgust and bled as much acid in his tone.

Rosalyn sniffed as tears pattered down. "Please listen—"

"How *dare* you betray my heart?" seared the Harlequin at Rosalyn. "There, I discovered you, laid in his bed, tumbled up in his sheets. He only mere paces away. Go," the Harlequin waved, "go shout for him. Shout out his name. I'm sure you already had *earlier*, wrapped up in his covers."

Rosalyn's jaw dropped at the accusation. She was such a flurry of emotions, she didn't know which one to pick.

Her mind spinning like a top, she whimpered out, "I ...
I love you—"

"*THEN LOVE ME!*" roared the Harlequin with a cruel
and demanding shrill to his voice.

Rosalyn broke down and wrapped her arms around
the Harlequin's tense neck. She couldn't stop sobbing.

The Harlequin's face was still and unfeeling as he gazed
ahead.

"Call for your Ruthless Sire, maiden." The Harlequin
disappeared.

Rosalyn dropped to the ground hard on her rump. The
woods were dark, all the golden orbs burned out in
shattering sparks raining down. Rosalyn covered her face
as the golden bits of light fell, she didn't know if they
would burn her as they flittered to the ground.

Rosalyn cried, "Harlequin! *Please*, I'm so sorry! Please
come back!"

"Rosalyn!" called Devonté. His cellphone light danced
wildly in the forest as he ran up to her, his headphones
pounding against his collarbones. He pumped out more
speed when he saw her mourning body.

Rosalyn looked up terrified. "No, no, no," she begged
as her brother ran up to her. "Leave me here! Leave me
here!" She covered her teary face from the dancing light.

Devonté tried to pick her up but Rosalyn fought
against him viciously. She thrashed about and flailed in
sheer protest.

"Leave me *here*! Leave me here!" Rosalyn demanded.
"Don't take me! *No!*" She scrambled out of his arms and
crawled away from him, the woodsy floor biting into her
palms. "I want to stay here!"

Devonté stood there, baffled. He had never seen Rosalyn so punchy. Her meltdowns were usually tears and screaming. This was new.

"*Harlequin!*" Rosalyn rang out. She broke into more tears, "Take-take me away—"

Devonté tried to clap a hand over her mouth and pick her up. She thrashed harder and even gnashed her teeth several times in vain effort to bite him. She got a bit of his pinky finally and he snatched his hand away. Mouth freed, Rosalyn ripped out a terrible scream that rang the night. Devonté flinched from the sheer volume, his ears were left ringing.

"I for*got* you had pipes," grunted Devonté as he tried to get a decent hand on her. He fell from a well-aimed pushing kick on his thigh as he kneeled. It took his leg clean out from under him and winded him.

"Harley," Rosalyn whimpered as she crawled backwards from her brother across the bramble. She couldn't get far, more lights were upon her. Rosalyn covered her eyes and turned her sobbing head away.

"Rosie? *Rosie!*" yelled her mother and father as they rushed to her. They could see Devonté trying to pick himself up off the ground with their flashlights.

Defeated, Rosalyn balled up and simply bawled into her lap.

Winston asked, stumped, "She had a meltdown out here? How'd she even get *past* us?"

Demetria tried to get some kind of control over her daughter's meltdown.

"Rosalyn," she said firmly but with care. Rosalyn's meltdowns were tricky, there was no one clear defined solution except for time — which they rarely had. "Rose, I know you're upset but we can't be out here," Demetria explained as she carefully approached her sobbing daughter. They heard her scream from inside the house, no one wanted to hear it up close.

Devonté ears still rang as his father helped him up.

"Devonté," huffed Winston, "what caused all of this? Wasn't she in your room sleeping? How did she get out here and so far?"

Devonté grunted as he rose up and leaned on his father. His chest panged; he struggled to get his breath and he could hardly hear over the ringing. He tried the best he could to talk, "I musta been ... too focused ... on my game. I looked back ... and she was ... gone." He tested his kicked leg, it shot with pain. He winced, "I found her out here ... and ... and tried to bring her back in. And, welp," he threw his free arm towards his balled-up sister, "she blew into pieces."

Demetria had less cooperation and she grew less patient. Nothing made her feel like an unfit mother quite like Rosalyn's meltdowns, *especially* if they were in public. They were much better to be avoided to save the stress and headache. But now, it was time to deal with the storm that was her frantic, teary daughter.

"Rose," directed Demetria flatly, "you are going to have to pull yourself *together*." She was a steady half yard away, ready for anything. "We are going back in the house—"

Rosalyn shrieked into her lap and cried louder.

Demetria winced from the sharp pitch of her loud wail but she remained firm. "We are going *back*. You can either walk or your father will carry you. You can get as mad as you like but we are *not* staying out here. It is not *safe*. You are upset, I get it, but we can't stay here. We can camp here over the summer but right now, we are going in the house."

Winston checked with his son, "You good, champ? Looks like I'm going to have to carry her in."

Devonté's leg ribbed with agony and his ribcage throbbed but he could manage. "I'm good, Dad. Just be careful with her." Devonté lifted off his father and stood on his own two feet. He checked his headphones, they miraculously stayed around his neck and remained unbroken. He picked up his phone from the groundcover and started his hobbled way back to the house.

Winston clapped and told Demetria, "Allow me. C'mon, baby girl." He walked over to Demetria and handed her his flashlight. "You gotta go inside, baby girl," he cooed as he approached Rosalyn.

When he picked her up, Rosalyn whined and sobbed. She tried to wriggle out of his grip but he was much too strong.

"I wanna *stay—*"

"I know you do," assured Winston, "but Momma's orders, we all gotta go back inside. You're going to be fine, we just have to head back inside."

Rosalyn dropped her head on her father's shoulder and wept openly as everyone left the woods.

Devonté was the first out of the woods. He could see lights on in the neighboring houses and even some standing on their back porches as he limped past.

Devonté yelled out with a wave, "Everything is fine! My sister fell and busted her ankle in the woods. Everything is good!"

Winston left the line of trees next with Rosalyn quietly whimpering in his arms and Demetria not too far behind. He yelled to everyone behind his son, "It's fine! Sorry for disturbing everybody's night. My daughter's fine!"

An elderly woman standing on her back porch called back, "I had called the police, you don't need them, right?"

Winston chuckled, "Nah, nah, no! Thank you, though!"

Demetria apologized to the woman, "Sorry to scare you!"

The old woman waved, "It's fine!" She headed back inside.

Tired and worn out, the Davis family entered their house, as did the other neighbors.

As the Davis family entered their home, Demetria instructed her husband, "Put her on our bed. Devonté, you ok?"

"I'm good, Ma," replied Devonté over Rosalyn's crying as he held the back door open for everyone. He then closed it and locked the door. *What a* night, he thought.

Up the stairs the family went. Devonté went to his room, his parents went to theirs. Rosalyn whined and struggled futilely in her father's arms as he carried her into the room.

Winston deposited Rosalyn on to his and Demetria's bed. She would have scampered away but Demetria caught her quickly and held her to the bed. Rosalyn loudly resisted but Demetria held firm as she tried to demand some sense into her daughter.

Winston blew out a heavy breath at the sight of the commotion and then visited Devonté. This was *not* the night he wanted to have.

He poked his head inside his son's room and knocked on the door, "Devonté? You wanna talk, son?"

Devonté was laid out across the bed, his feet firm on the floor, arms crossed over his face. His body blared with pain but it was nothing sleep couldn't mend. His head still reeled from the fighting and his heart still hammered from the adrenaline. He looked at his father and sat up to nod.

Winston came in, closed the door and sat beside him. They could hear Rosalyn's pips of cries from the end of the hall as Demetria tried to calm her.

Winston shook his head and chuckled out a heavy breath, "Man, we *really* need this vacation — oh, your mother told you, right? We're going to the sea this weekend, Diamond Beach."

Devonté nodded, "Yeah, Mom told me." He dropped his head, "I'm sorry things got out of hand, Dad—"

"No. No," Winston raised a finger. He thought something was up when Devonté dashed out of the kitchen door, the later scream confirmed it. "Do *not* apologize. Don't. I am not raising a man who apologizes for doing the right thing, for looking out for his little sister. It just means I raised you *right*."

Devonté tried to smile and feel proud but he couldn't. His father put an arm over him and patted his arm.

"*Never* apologize for taking care of your family," expressed Winston. "Especially your little sister. She's *always* going to need you. There are a *lot* of crazy men out here with nothin' — and I mean *nothin'* — but bad intentions for her. Ain't nothin' change since I was a boy. I fought day and night for your aunt and especially for your uncle when he came out. Some men are just *reckless*. And that was here in New Tulsa, son. It's *worse* out there. Things have changed a little but they don't change a lot. You will *always* have to look out for your sister."

Devonté nodded. If only his dad knew even *half* the tale.

Winston patted Devonté's shoulder, "I sometimes don't know what we're going to do with your sister. Always in her room, always in her head, always in her books — it … it worries me. She just simply doesn't seem interested in living in reality at all. I don't want her to put the books down, she loves them so much … I just want her to look around at least once in a while."

From down the hall, they heard Rosalyn plead and bawl, "I don't *wanna* go to the sea, Mommy! I wanna stay *here!*"

Winston squeezed the bridge of his nose and fettered out a breathy laugh. "She really doesn't have a choice. And maybe a change in scenery will be good for her."

Chapter 9

Beach Day had arrived. Demetria, Winston and Devonté couldn't be more ready. Since the forest meltdown, there was a new rule to never let Rosalyn out of anyone's sight and to keep her away from her books. Instead, she had to watch television. Devonté tried to find some dramas from Korea and Japan that could possibly pique her interest but she passionately hated them all.

Demetria and Winston allowed Devonté to stay home from class for the rest of the week to keep a close eye on his sister. It was meltdown after meltdown. Especially when she learned she could only sleep in her parents' room or her brother's room when it was time for bed.

Every day, the family basically relived the forest meltdown at least once a day. Everyone, including Rosalyn, was frazzled down to their last nerve.

On vacation day, the family tried to pile into the SUV at four in the morning. Keyword: tried.

Demetria ticked on the beside lamp to its softest setting as her phone alarm vibrated next to her cream red satin pillow. She didn't dare use a sound alarm, Rosalyn slept in their bed between her and Winston. Winston's phone also vibrated its alarm.

Rosalyn was a fitful sleeper, hardly anyone got any rest when she shared their bed. But it was better than letting her be in her room.

Both Winston and Demetria silenced their alarms and got up slow and cautious to avoid waking Rosalyn. But Rosalyn stirred awake all the same. Demetria and Winston sighed at the impending storm waiting for them and hoped it would not be any time soon.

The parents let Rosalyn rest for a little while longer as they got dressed in their large bedroom. Their king-sized bed sat in the middle of the room, covered in the coral brown sheets that matched the heavy drapes on their windows. The drapes were pulled back with gold corded ties. There was an ivory, Rococo-styled armoire and matching make up desk by the door, opposite from the foot of the bed. Demetria's make up consumed most of the top of the desk in small bundles or bottles but Winston beard oil and moisturizer lived there also among the beauty clutter. The mirror that sat on the make-up desk towered tall, the top was only a few feet from the vaulted ceiling.

Their room was neat for the most part but there still were some misplaced ties and high-heel pumps scattered about. The closet that lived on the right-hand side of the room was split into a His and Hers arrangement. Demetria's clothes and shoes on the right, Winston's clothes and shoes on the left. Rosalyn had a few pieces of her own hanging in the middle, all picked a few days ago by Demetria. The clothes were there so Rosalyn couldn't have a plausible excuse to go into her room and possibly barricade herself in. No one wanted to relive that. She already had tried earlier during the week.

Winston and Demetria were dressed. They both had on simple outfits. No point in being fancy, it was early in the morning and they had to deal with Rosalyn next.

Demetria and Winston already agreed ahead of time to not dress Rosalyn, just get her to the car with as little meltdown as possible.

Demetria wore a navy blue sailor top and white capris. She patted her husband's shoulder and kissed him on the cheek. "I'll go check on Devonté. Good luck with Rosie."

Winston sighed in his dark salmon shirt and khaki pants. "I'll try." He kissed his wife and turned to the bed as Demetria left the bedroom.

"Ooooooookay, Rosalyn," Winston prepped himself as he looked down upon his slumbering and not-currently-noisy daughter. "Gotta get you on this trip. Hopefully it won't kill us both."

The past week, he learned he got less fuss out of her if she stayed in her nightgown. Check.

The rest?

Purely up to luck.

Winston leaned down and pulled back the covers cautiously.

Eyes closed, Rosalyn uttered out a light whine but nothing worse than that.

So far, so good.

Winston bent down and cradled his youngest into his arms. She stirred in his arms as he carefully rose her from the bed.

"Harley?" Rosalyn feathered out by her father's ear.

Winston sighed. He had no idea how a book crush could have such an effect on her.

"Nope, sorry," he gently replied. "No Harley. But there will be sea, sand and fresh air."

Rosalyn's face crumpled into a disparaging frown as her eyes remained shut. She was sunken in drowsiness but she didn't want to be anywhere her Harlequin wasn't. How could she regain his trust in her? He still hadn't visited her since the forest.

One of her legs ticked, she started to motion her shoulders in a slight wiggle.

"Oh, no, no, no," Winston defied quietly as he kept hold on her like a wily fish soon to wriggle out of his grasp. "No, you don't." He kissed her forehead. Her face ticked a wince and she began to whine and shift a little more.

She was starting up, Winston could tell.

Better deliver her to the car quick.

As Winston ambled towards the door with his resistive daughter, Winston cooed, "Ah, ah, ah. You're gonna have so much fun."

Rosalyn cracked open her eyes a little, and tears began to collect.

Winston sighed and just held his daughter even tighter. She gave a bit of a kick when they passed the closed and locked door of her room but Winston held firm.

Together, they ambled down the stairs and through the open front door. Demetria waited by the SUV, headlights on and engine running. The car doors were all open, except for Devonté's. Devonté was buckled in and fast asleep. His headphones rested around his neck as they played video game concertos, his darkened phone sat in his lap. He was playing a mobile game but drifted back to sleep. He had on a black shirt and olive shorts.

Demetria had already filled the car with their luggage and collected Devonté. Rosalyn was the only one left — and the only one in bed clothes, which suited everyone just fine at this point. Anything to avoid a meltdown.

Demetria walked up to her husband and wriggling daughter, car keys in hand. She pecked Winston on the cheek and said gently, "Devvi's in the car. I'll turn out the lights and lock up, you put her in the car."

Winston nodded and proceeded to the car as Demetria went back inside. Rosalyn whimpered on his shoulder and tried to swing her calves as Winston took her to the open back seat door on the passenger side. He slid her in with a bit of a thump, waking Devonté.

Devonté saw who was beside him and tried to reach for the seatbelt Winston struggled to pull over Rosalyn. It was difficult to keep her seated and pull the belt over her, she wouldn't stop wriggling.

Winston kept her seated back with an arm across her shoulders. She tried to press forward against her father's arm and cranked out a weeping whine in vain while Devonté reached over her to receive the buckle from his father and buckle her in.

Buckled in finally, Devonté grabbed his sister's wrists and bundled them together so she couldn't undo her seatbelt. Rosalyn tried to tug her arms away, steady streams of tears now running down her cheeks to accompany her whines, but Devonté quietly held firm. He tried to settle himself back in with her wrists in his hands, sighing annoyed. He didn't want to ignore her tears but it was early morning, he was tired and hated waking early. It was still nighttime, as far as he was concerned.

Seeing her properly restrained but unhappy, Winston shut the car door like a beleaguered cop. He had never seen his daughter so resistive before. She used to love beach trips.

"You gotta *chill*, Rose," warned Devonté as she sniffed and struggled.

She wanted to stay home. She wanted her Harlequin.

House dark and front door locked, Demetria and Winston entered the front seats and buckled in.

Demetria could hear the struggle and whimpers behind her as she grasped the steering wheel and placed her foot on the brake. She sighed, simply too tired to say anything.

Instead, she just focused on putting the car in reverse and started to back out the driveway. Raising teenagers could be such a headache and a half.

Everyone hoped this would be the extent of her morning meltdown.

Rosalyn eventually simmered down into sleep not too long after. She tired herself out as she fussed and struggled to wrest her hands free from Devonté. She didn't want to be touched, she wanted the Harlequin's trust back.

But Devonté held firm. He wanted to bundle herself into his arms in a big hug so he could have an easier time keeping ahold of her and get some sleep but he knew that would cause a bigger eruption than they already had on their hands.

No one wanted that.

Thus, he held on, fighting sleep to keep his sister's hands down until she drifted off herself. He eventually got what he wanted twenty minutes later. He checked her knelt head to be sure. Against the reddening line of sunrise over the flat hills they drove past, Devonté saw Rosalyn's silhouette. Her eyes were closed, her breath was calm.

Devonté sighed and slid his hands off her. He gave her temple a light peck and sat back to drift off himself.

The drive was quicker than everyone thought. The map said it was supposed to be an hour but thanks to the clear roads of the early morning, it was more like forty-five minutes. They also stayed away from passing through downtown, where there were still occasional skirmishes from outsiders.

It was a bit scary but it was nothing the town couldn't handle, that's what the sleeper reserves were for. Devonté saw that when he briefly checked his friends' stream playbacks as he got dressed. Jumper had new toys he cooked up to share with the Thunder Twins, a special drone that could self-direct air strikes made of capsicum-mixed paintballs at anything that had a Confederate flag, Gadsden flag, or a person wearing a Hawaiian shirt who could pass the paper bag test. Fun times.

Devonté was grateful he was a New Tulsan. No place like home.

The glittering sea in the full moonlight captivated Demetria. She loved the sights as she drove by on the winding road. There were no longer trees, hills, and forestry, but sands and wildflowers running past. The brisk, salty warm air soothed her nerves and filled her with ease. She took in a lung full of fresh sea air and sighed.

They all needed the trip.

The beach house sat behind the lip of the stony wall that oversaw the beach and the piers. The house sat in a short row of three Victorian sea homes, all meant for renting. Every house bore restored wooden slats and stood about three stories tall. Each house had steepled roofs, complete with a diamond-styled weathervane that idly rotated in the breeze. The driveways were all empty; the other two houses hadn't been rented. Only the dusk blue one in the middle, where Demetria pulled in slowly. The headlights momentarily bathed the home in blinding ivory rings of light that shrank down on the wall until they lightly bounced from the soft stop of the car.

Demetria parked in the driveway and got out her phone to pull up the key app for the house. She made sure everyone had it on their phone earlier this week. (She installed it on Rosalyn's phone herself as Rosalyn slept a couple nights ago.) Demetria planned to relax and be wholly unbothered during the beach trip. A jacuzzi in the basement, a sea-side view, a hammock on the second-floor balcony, Demetria planned to absorb as much serenity as she could during this short time.

She nudged Winston awake and checked the back. Both kids were fast asleep.

"Get Rosalyn in first, nice and easy," Demetria whispered. "There's a room on the second floor. All the rooms face the sea."

Winston nodded and with a little metallic click, he unbuckled as Demetria did the same. They both left the car as silently as they could. Demetria went up to the house and climbed the cement stairs. She unlocked the black wooden double doors with the back of her phone laid against the keyhole drawing above the locks by tapping a small, matching keyhole symbol on her screen. The locks clanked open electronically and her screen flashed:

Arrived! Enjoy Your Stay!
Guests: 4
Key Privileges: 4

They were now all checked in and all their phones could control the doors. Demetria smiled and let herself in to explore the house. She was eager to make the most of her vacation, every second of it.

As Demetria handled the door and check in, Winston went to carefully open the car door on Rosalyn's side and unbuckle her seatbelt. Her head was slumped, face obscured by her mop of hair. Seatbelt carefully pulled back soundlessly, Winston gave himself a silent prayer and proceeded to slip his arms behind her back and under her legs. She was lifeless as he gathered her against himself. His daughter's head laid on his shoulder, Winston turned around and carried her up the cement stairs and through the front doors Demetria left open for him. She waited inside with her phone's flashlight beaming when she heard his footsteps.

The house was dark and smelled of saccharine apples and cinnamon. Demetria lit the way with her flashlight. No one wanted to turn on the light and risk waking Rosalyn.

Up the stairs the trio traveled until they found the first bedroom. It was small and filled with countless nautical motifs. Nets, decorative lifesavers, plastic fishes, the room carried a playful feel. The moonlight shone brightly in through the tall window. A small lifesaver dangled on the end of the long string from the curled-up window shade.

The bed was plain and tiny. It had a cheap, black metal frame that sat on tiny black wheels. The bed looked a bit old-timey. A crocheted yellow blanket sat folded up at the end of the bed. Moonlight bathed the entire bed in its silvery glow.

"Rosalyn will love this," breathed Demetria softly with a gentle smile.

"I hope so," sighed Winston just as gently. Like a fragile crystal, he brought Rosalyn to the bed and laid her down in the moonlight. She slept peacefully, head lolled to the side, lips lightly parted.

The transfer was complete.

Demetria and Winston kissed each other on a job well done. Demetria then closed the door silently to continue moving into their snug vacation home.

They both went back downstairs to get Devonté. He was much, much easier. A simple tap on the shoulder and steer up the stairs was all it took. Once he was in bed in his room, which bore more of an antique nautical scene, the parents marched off to bed themselves.

All was quiet until morning.

Rosalyn was the first to wake up. She hated the place the moment she opened her eyes. The room was so unfamiliar and empty of books. She looked out of the window and saw the morning sea washing in. That was one consolation to her, the ocean looked lovely and majestic. She looked down and saw a black asphalt road that wound behind the houses, the stubby stone wall, and little wooden docks meant for small boats. A wooden walkway spanned along the docks beside the asphalt road, split by the wall. The piers jutted out into the sea from the walkway like the teeth of a wide comb. Wooden crates stacked up in threes dotted along the docks and road. There was a triplet of crates almost directly below.

It was all so captivating to Rosalyn — but she still wanted to go home. She left her room and surveyed the rest of the house. Everything seemed so fanciful, nautical and old. She knew she would have loved it if it were under other circumstances but she missed the Harlequin too much. She wanted to make things right with him. She touched her necklace, lovesick and forlorn.

Although, the more Rosalyn looked, the more the house grew on her. The classical nature was what warmed her up most.

She came across everyone's luggage piled in the center of the living room. Her bag was a tiny, stuffed, grey gingham overnight bag packed by her mother earlier that week. She remembered how she cried and begged not to go as her mother filled the bag on Rosalyn's bed. The moment Demetria stepped out to grab a toothbrush in the bathroom, Rosalyn slammed the door behind her and tried to barricade the door with her body. It took Winston and

Devonté to get the door open and extract a screaming, kicking Rosalyn out of it.

Rosalyn felt a flush of embarrassment at the memory and went to get the bag. It had a decent weight to it but she could carry it with a single shoulder. She still had on her nightgown. It was washed thoroughly after she was found in the woods. Then the nightgown was locked away in a closet for a couple days after that, Rosalyn had to beg and plead with her parents to get it back. She hated modern sleeping clothes, they weren't delicate and fanciful enough.

Rosalyn placed the bag on the floor to open it wider. She fished out a short-sleeved shirt dotted with black stars and a pair of olive pedal pushers. She happened across a pair of sparkle, clear jelly sandals and sat down to put them on her bare feet. She then slipped on the pedal pushers under her nightgown and then took off her nightgown to put on her star shirt. She felt a small phantom kiss on the side of her lower back. It made her jump and whirl around, her heart aflutter.

She hadn't felt any phantom touches, good or bad, since she last encountered the Harlequin. The room was empty but she still smiled. He hadn't fully abandoned her.

Rosalyn threw on the shirt and fluffed out her hair. Her mother tried to wash and braid it the day before but Rosalyn resisted too much with another meltdown. The entire kitchen was soaked, them included.

Rosalyn searched over the luggage pile until she found a few bloated bundles of blue grocery bags. She picked through the bags until she found a nice cold cut sandwich wrapped up and still with a deli sticker on it. It had a bit of leftover chill in her hand, the sandwich was pulled from the refrigerator right before the family left. The groceries were from Winston's shopping the day prior. He thought it had rained inside the house when he saw all the water in the kitchen and some slashes of water stains in the living room on the couch, television and walls.

She unwrapped the sandwich and took a bite from one end.

"Good morning," greeted Devonté from behind Rosalyn. She gave a bit of a jump and whirled around, chewing. He stood a couple meters away, hopeful for an easy morning. He wore his Sankofa Chocobo shirt, some old bleach-stained basketball shorts and black sports slippers. "You're up early."

She looked at the sandwich and offered it to her brother. She tried to ignore if it was okay or not.

Sports slippers clapping against the wooden floor, Devonté came over and took a bite.

"It's really good," Rosalyn commented. The olives really brought the flavors together and the spicy spread was delightful with its traces of chipotle and wasabi.

Devonté nodded, "Yeah, it is." He swallowed and then asked, "How ya feelin'?"

Rosalyn knew what that meant: Is there another storm coming?

"I'm fine," she answered softly into the sandwich.

Devonté sighed and rubbed his head. "Look, I know you miss … him," Devonté gestured to the great outdoors beyond, "but try to enjoy the trip, okay? At *least* try not to fight any of us?" He pulled his phone from his pocket and booted up a mobile game. "I'mma be outside. Come to the ocean with me."

Rosalyn shrank into herself and shook her head no. She took another bite.

Devonté sighed yet again, more haggard this time, "Look, Rozay. You know you can't be left by yourself, not even on this trip. Ain't nothin' gonna happen to you, just c'mon … please? I don't wanna be cooped up in this old house all day. There isn't even a TV." He took Rosalyn by the hand, he could feel her tug back. "Please?"

Rosalyn didn't feel like she had much choice. Everything she encountered felt like a debate for a fight. She just wanted to be with her Harlequin. After a moment of pensive quiet, she answered, "…okay."

Devonté smiled and pecked her on the cheek, which made her flinch. He then led her to the side door that divided the wooden kitchen from the living room, graced with a square window that showed the white slats of the next house. It opened with a springy creak.

The warm salty sea air greeted them both. The sky was blue but gray clouds sailed across. Lapping waves and squawking seagulls filled the air around them. Diamond Beach was a small but restful place. Dotted with a few summer houses and a little supermarket up the road, it was a tiny, slow sea-faring New Tulsan spot. Top relaxation location for those who wanted to get away from the city without ever having to leave the safety of the community.

Together, Devonté and Rosalyn went down the triplet of whitewashed wooden stairs. They crossed the narrow asphalt road to get to the wooden walkway through one of the wide gaps in the stone wall. As they crossed the road,

Devonté texted both of his parents: "Rose is w me. No freakouts".

Devonté spotted the crates. He thought they looked cool, like something out of a game. He pointed, intrigued, "'Ey, let's take a picture there!"

Rosalyn was unsure. "I … I …."

Devonté raised an eyebrow. "Rose, c'mon. You can't let him dictate your every move!" He pulled her to the crates, "One picture, one picture!"

Rosalyn clodded along as she tried to twist her arm out of his grip.

Devonté plopped down on the crate and sat his sister on his lap. Rosalyn looked around, she didn't want to make a scene. No one was around but she was still outside. Outside always had people somewhere. She was so tired of everyone fighting her. She didn't like her meltdowns either but she didn't really know how to keep them from coming. They always appeared like awful storms she couldn't stop, only avoid.

Her brother turned on the front facing camera and posed his cellphone far above them. Rosalyn laid her head against her brother and tried to give a feeble smile for the camera. Devonté threw up a palm-outward peace sign and took the picture.

Once the picture was taken, Rosalyn immediately hopped off Devonté's lap and shrank into herself. Devonté checked the picture and pocketed his phone. It wasn't a bad shot. At least Rosalyn tried to smile.

"See?" Devonté beamed. "Wasn't that bad." He got up to grab her by her clasped hands, "Let's sit at the end of the dock."

He led her to the very end of the dock as if he were pulling an obstinate mule. They sat down, legs dangling over.

Devonté continued his gaming as Rosalyn looked out into the sea. The sky had gotten a little grayer.

As he collected jeweled cherries before an evil groundhog could eat them up in a candy cane maze, Devonté asked, "How long have you known him?"

Rosalyn paled at the question. She bundled her hands into her lap and bowed her head.

Devonté repeated himself, focused on his game, "How long? Since when? Is this, like, some crazy 'Pagemaster' bull or what?"

Rosalyn didn't want to answer. No one wanted to understand, only force and degrade. Rosalyn looked away at the sea and fingered her necklace. The gray sea surged back and forth.

Devonté noticed. "Is that necklace from him?"

Rosalyn jumped, her blood ran cold. She whipped her head away and rushed out, "Don't take it from me—"

"Whoa, whoa, whoa," Devonté threw up his hands, astonished. "I ain't say I was gonna snatch it. I just asked if it was his. I guess so, given how you're acting."

Rosalyn stared at him with fearful eyes, a hand clasped firm over her necklace. She breathed heavily until words found her. "Why won't *any* of you leave me *alone*—"

"He is *twisting* your head up and you need to *see* that," Devonté lobbed back. He went back to his gaming. "He literally leaves you with cuts—"

"Because he thinks I'm not faithful to him!" Rosalyn's voice rose to near booming. She checked her volume and shrank back into herself, a hand still over her necklace.

Devonté couldn't believe what he was hearing. He paused his game to look at her, completely deadpan. "Are you seriously *saying* that? Are you even *hearing* yoursel—"

"You don't under*stan*—"

"I'm tryna understand why some psycho clown-lookin' demon—"

"Don't call him that!" Rosalyn started to burn up. The grey skies started to wash ashore more and more. A storm was coming.

"No? Okay, fine! Whatever you want to call him, he ain't good for you!" Devonté was at his wits' end. He sincerely wished he could get *through* to her. "He isn't! Do you even know what he wants to *do* with you?"

That was enough for Rosalyn. Her Harlequin wasn't like that. He was ethereal. Princely to her. He *loved* her.

She got up. "You're disgusting," she spat. "I'm going back inside." Rosalyn stormed down the pier, arms folded.

Floored, Devonté stayed there, frozen. He was truly gobsmacked. But soon, he got up and started to run after his sister.

Hearing his footsteps on the wooden floorboards, Rosalyn whirled around with a hand over her necklace to shout, "Don't follow me!" Once she saw Devonté slow to a stop, she turned back around, arms folded once more, and continued to storm back to the house.

Devonté pinched the bridge of his nose. He had no idea how to make things right.

Rosalyn came inside, burning with fury. Demetria and Winston were chatting away at the antique carved wooden table in the kitchen, holding hands and exchanging wistful memories when Rosalyn blew in. The living room was emptier now that the luggage and groceries were unpacked and put away.

Rosalyn stomped to the plush, grey-chocolate couch and threw herself down. She curled up facing towards the back cushions and kicked off her shoes. They fell to the floor with a resounding clatter.

Demetria and Winston watched her come in and lay down. They then looked at each other.

Devonté sped in not too long after. He spotted Rosalyn on the couch and looked around, spotting his parents.

Winston mouthed, "What happened?"

Devonté shook his head and raised a hand. He mouthed, "Let her sleep."

Demetria and Winston sighed and rubbed each other hands. So much for a calm and pleasant weekend.

Chapter 10

Nighttime fell. Rosalyn laid in bed. She had on her nightgown. She had to promise her parents no meltdowns just to even enter her room, let alone get her nightgown. They had a plain, honey brown summer pajama set ready for her. It was a little button-up with shorts and a small teddy bear on the breast pocket. It took everything in her to not have a meltdown at that.

She got up to look out the window. The sky had a few clusters of clouds scattered about but the moon still hung bright. The clouds still gathered, though. They had been on and off all day. Threatening and then not.

The sea rippled and sloshed ashore. The waves glittered like stars under the moonlight. Rosalyn touched her necklace. She then looked down.

On the crates below sat the Harlequin. He raised his clawed hand in a regal greeting, as if toasting to her. He had on a kind smile.

Rosalyn couldn't believe her eyes. She threw on her jellies she had brought upstairs and tipped out of the room.

Before she reached the stairs, she heard around her, *Close your eyes and wish for me.*

A smile sneaked onto her face. Rosalyn closed her eyes and touched her necklace. She wished for the Harlequin with all her heart. The air changed around her, from saccharine and cool to salty and warm. The waves sounded closer. Clawed hands clasped hers with care. She grasped them tight and adoringly.

"Open your eyes, Midnight Maiden," chuckled the Harlequin.

Opened them she did — and saw how she stood above the rippling waters of the ocean. No, she was *on* the water. A circle of calm waves surrounded them as the rest of the sea churned like normal around it. The Harlequin stood before her, smiling.

He kissed her. She kissed back. They both grinned at each other. Oh, how she missed him dearly.

Rosalyn looked for the shore, the sandy beach was about the distance of two Olympic-sized pools away. She looked back at the Harlequin, her heart swelled for him. Rosalyn laid her head against his chest ... and began to slowly sink.

Rosalyn grew panicked. She could see her feet become swallowed by the water like quicksand. She looked up desperately at the Harlequin, who only smiled sweetly at her.

She patted his chest and tried to step atop the water but kept sloshing through. "Harley, Harley, *please!*"

The Harlequin simply looked down upon her and continued smiling sweetly.

Rosalyn screamed as more and more of her legs sank under, "Harlequin, *please*! I'm *sorry*! I was made to do it! He made me! I love you! *I love you!*"

Her words fell on deaf ears. She continued sinking.

Devonté noticed his phone was running low on battery. He sat in his room listening to music as he played his mobile game. When he got off his bed to get his charger, he looked out the window — and saw his sister sinking into the sea at the feet of the Harlequin.

He had to do something.

Devonté padded out of his room and down the stairs as quietly and quickly as he could without alerting his parents. They were in their room at the end of the hall making the most out of their getaway weekend, shades drawn and door closed.

He threw his phone and headphones on the couch when he snuck past. As soon as Devonté reached the side door, he bolted like a shot to the sea.

Rosalyn was up to her throat in the ocean. She coughed and screeched, "I can't swim well! Don't do this to me, Harley!"

The Harlequin tilted his head as he stared at her with his unchanged smile. "If only you loved me only, you would be standing alongside me."

Rosalyn went under.

"Rosalyn!" screamed Devonté. He pumped his legs as hard as he could, his slippers flung off his feet as he ran. He used to be on the swim team back in high school before gaming really took over his life. He hoped he could still nail his old records.

Rosalyn sputtered up over the water. The Harlequin was gone. Her face crumpled into tears as she tried to tread water in her nightgown. She could barely keep her head above water, the undercurrents overwhelmed her. She coughed and sputtered as she accidentally breathed in some sea water. The bitter salt taste disgusted her and burned her throat.

"Harley!" she cried out before her head bobbed under once more.

Devonté swam as fast and hard as he could to Rosalyn. Water thrashed around him as he sliced through the waves. Devonté could tell there was a rip current, he used it to propel him faster to his sister. He could definitely tell he was out of practice but the adrenaline kept him at top speed.

He saw his sister struggling to keep her head above water. Devonté pushed to reach her faster and hoped the Harlequin wouldn't halt him like before. No telling what that ethereal maniac would do.

Devonté reached Rosalyn. He tried to loop an arm under her but she kept panicking.

"I got you!" Devonté commanded at the top of his lungs, "Stop moving and hold on to me, I got you!"

Rosalyn calmed her thrashing enough for Devonté to thread an arm under her arms but she still wailed loudly as he swam her diagonally to shore. The current fought him but Devonté didn't let up. But his body desperately wanted to.

Beleaguered, Devonté paddled the best he could to shore. He battled not to give up. All the things the Harlequin could do in this instance kept him going.

It took a few dogged minutes for them to reach shore. Devonté had never been so drained and worn out in all his life as he dragged his sister onto the sandy shore.

She still wailed, occasionally sobbing for breath. She couldn't believe the Harlequin did this to her. How he merely smiled as she drowned, begging. She curled up in the sand and choked out more tears. Then soon, she was silent.

Devonté had never felt woozier. He stumbled and fell backwards into the sand, dead asleep.

Rosalyn woke up to the morning sun in her room under her blanket. Phantom kisses crowded her lips, neck and heart.

Please forgive me, whispered around her. *Find me in the woods, Midnight Maiden.* One more phantom kiss graced her lips. She felt a clawed hand squeeze her hand. She looked down, there was nothing there.

Devonté woke up in his bed. His sandy, soggy slippers surrounded his head on his pillow. The last he remembered was pulling Rosalyn out of the water—

He bounced out of his bed and dashed into her room. Upon finding her, Devonté threw himself down upon her bed to wrap his arms around her and hug her tight.

"Thank God, thank God," he whispered into her shoulder.

She was lifeless in his hug. Rosalyn wanted him off her.

"I'm fine. Thank you," said Rosalyn without emotion. She asked, "Can you make me breakfast?" Anything to get him off her and not talk about last night.

Grateful that she was alright and rather famished himself, Devonté wholeheartedly agreed, "Yeah, sure. I think we might have pancake mix." He took her by the hand and together they went downstairs.

Chapter 11

After breakfast, packing began. Today was the last day of vacation and no one was happier about it than Rosalyn. She packed and piled her things into the car the fastest. Her bubbling mirth did not go unnoticed by the rest of her family. It worried them. She was ecstatic now ... what about later, though?

But Winston had an idea he shared to his family inside the house as Rosalyn waited eagerly in the car: "Let her be in the woods today, as long as it's daytime. We can't just ban her, she'll just ricochet in there harder. If she can handle herself, we can let up."

On the drive home, Winston presented his idea as he drove.

"Ok, Rosalyn, listen up and listen well," announced Winston as he sailed the car down the winding beach roads back into town, "When we get home, you *will* be allowed back in the woods — But! With stipulations: Daytime *only*. It gets dark, you get inside. Understood?"

Rosalyn agreed, eager, "Yes, Daddy."

"Two: You won't be supervised but you better expect checks. The more you act up, the more frequent they'll be until you won't be allowed back in the woods at *all* until next summer. Understood?"

Rosalyn nodded again, "Yes, Daddy." She could barely hide her delight. She fingered her necklace, which laid proudly above the scoop neck of her ribbed, yellow short sleeved shirt. Devonté noticed as he played his mobile game with his headphones off.

"Three: Dress for the environment, not for the style. Normal clothes only. I know you love feeling like a lost princess prancing in the woods in your nightgown but it's not designed for that. Sleeping & lounging only in the nightgown. Regular clothes for the outdoors. Understood?"

Rosalyn nodded, brimming with a wide, toothy smile, "Yes, Daddy."

"Four: If you handle today well, you can sleep in your own room and start to work back your night privileges. Is that clear?"

"Okay, Daddy," she buzzed with immense joy.

Demetria and Devonté hoped this wouldn't backfire. Everyone was gone during the day due to school and work so this basically ran on the honor system. But it was better than nothing and far better than facing meltdown after meltdown.

Once home, Rosalyn couldn't dart into the woods fast enough. She ripped out of the car the moment it stopped.

Demetria wanted to call her back to get her bags but Devonté already had hers and his slung over his shoulders.

It wasn't long before Rosalyn reached the river.

"Harley!" she called out. "I'm here!"

Nothing.

Her joy dampened a little. She called out again, "Harlequin?"

Cross the river and find me, Midnight Maiden, the wind whispered around her.

Rosalyn stared at the burbling, surging river. It was about three meters across and filled with slippery rocks. A few stood out the water, gray and jaunty. She remembered her tries during the winter. How cold the water sliced, the agonizing slips—

She had to try. She didn't want to lose the Harlequin again. Rosalyn wanted to show her trust and faith in him. Her love for him.

The river proved as daunting as she had remembered from the winter. The first rock she had set her jelly-slippered foot upon was a dry, flat rock that gave almost as soon as she placed half her weight on it. The rock raced down the river, taken by the current.

Rosalyn watched the rock knock about down the river. It wasn't deep, the river only went up to her hips, but it was full of very slippery things she could hit her head on—

She had to try. She had to show trust and loyalty. To earn her love back.

Rosalyn looked for a different dry rock to try. There was indeed another, almost a small boulder about a yard away. It was far rounder than the flat top rock she tried. And bigger, she was certain she would have to jump on it.

But she had to try. She had to prove her love.

Rosalyn took a couple steps back and tried to mentally measure the jump. She had no idea if the rock would give or what she would do if she missed the shot. But Rosalyn was willing to try.

She ran and leapt.

And never landed on the rock.

Instead, Rosalyn remained suspended in the air, weightless. Before her appeared the Harlequin on the other side of the bank. He smiled as his arms remained outstretched. Slowly, Rosalyn descended to him, a bright smile plastered across her face.

She landed in his arms, safe and sound.

Rosalyn was so overcome with a rupture of joyous emotions, the tears came flowing. She laid her head upon the Harlequin's chest.

"Oh, Harley," she breathed. She nestled deep into his arms and held him tightly. He enclosed his arms around her in deep embrace as well.

Then Rosalyn felt something change about her. The threads of her clothes started to rearrange until they wove themselves into a beautiful, delicate gown.

As it wove, the Harlequin expressed, "Something to most suit you, my dear Midnight Maiden. Already you visit me in the sun at my request. How honored I am that you should grace me with your adoring presence. Even as the Ruthless Sire and his little army tries to fill you with lies. He wants to drive us far apart. To keep you for himself. To be *selfish* and *controlling*. Is this the love you want? Is it? To cage you and drive you away from whatever *he* dislikes? To do as *he* sees fit? No matter your choice?"

The Harlequin lifted up Rosalyn's chin to his face and gave her a light kiss. Her hair began to dot with golden stars. A small chain laid upon her crown. It ran down the center part as a small golden diamond pendant rested against her forehead.

The Harlequin continued, "Don't you want to keep him from driving us apart? He is the terror of the night, you are the stars."

The gown was done, it was a delicate ivory and gold chemise with a subtle diamond pattern traveling up from the hem. She noticed that she was bare underneath, something that usually made her deeply uncomfortable but she willed the discomfort away.

The Harlequin planted another kiss on her and stepped back to adore her dressings. He was in awe.

"I can only hope the goddess of the night smiles upon my gift to one of Her most glorious daughters as She slumbers," marveled the Harlequin.

Rosalyn thought the chemise was gorgeous as well but she couldn't help but wish for undergarments.

The Harlequin kneeled before Rosalyn, "I ask most humbly to be taken in by the night that is your skin." He bowed his head.

Rosalyn blushed. She didn't know what to say. Her head was a blur of feelings … so she said, "Yes."

The Harlequin lifted his head, a hungry smile curled across his face.

As he stood up, Rosalyn was floated backwards slowly until she hovered in midair, the groundcover loosely floated beneath her.

The Harlequin looked upon her adoringly as he stroked her head. He then kissed her deeply. Rosalyn tried to be as receptive as she could to his embrace. She wanted to push down any drifting, bubbling feeling of unsureness but they kept surging back.

As he kissed her, the Harlequin took a claw from each hand and from the chemise's neckline, he traced a clean line down the curves of her shoulders. He broke the kiss and looked down adoringly at the chemise. He then looked back at Rosalyn and pinched the front of the chemise's shoulders. He neatly folded down the top half until her plunge was well revealed.

Rosalyn could feel the doubled over fabric laid over the full of her bust and her stomach. Her mind was blank. She didn't want this. But she wanted to show how much she loved and trusted him. She couldn't tell if he could see her shiver, she tried not to show it.

The Harlequin smiled a mischievous grin. He bent over and kissed her neck, traveling downward. He kissed her pendant and her heart countless times. He drifted shoulder to shoulder with kisses until he made his way further down towards her plunge. He stuck out a purple-pink tongue and laid it deep upon her plunge.

Rosalyn felt the smooth sliminess of the tongue between her breast and seized up. She didn't want this at all. Her head was like traveling light, she didn't know what to say or what to do. She emitted a small squeak in her discomfort, which made the Harlequin bring back in his tongue and slowly stand up, his face marked with clear, bored annoyance.

"I love you …" Rosalyn shivered, "… but … I'm-I'm not ready." She reached out for him, "Pl-please don't leave." Her hand shrank back to her side. She was sure he would be gone for good.

"You're not ready," repeated the Harlequin, his voice soaked with agitation. "Your heart swells for me, but it's not *ready*."

"I love you—"

"But you're not *ready*," reminded the Harlequin darkly.

Rosalyn thought for anything, any string of anything to grasp to. Anything to make him not disappear again.

"I … I am the Midni-Midnight Ma-maiden. Shou-shouldn't I at least-least be g-given the night?" Rosalyn offered. She didn't think she would be ready by nightfall but anything, *anything* to keep the Harlequin from abandoning her, even if it was only for a little while longer.

The Harlequin's irritation fell. She had a point.

With a hand passed over her top upwards, the Harlequin made her chemise whole as he realized, "To take you not under the glory of night would indeed be a disgrace to the wonderful, eternal goddess of the night." He stroked Rosalyn's head, "To become one with one of Her most illustrious of daughters as She sleeps— during when Her *daughter* should be sleeping— it's … it's …." The Harlequin turned his head away and covered his face with his claws, "Forgive me, most passionate maiden. How I so much desired the night of your skin, I truly forgot myself and my place. It is we who chase the night." He looked back at Rosalyn, voice filled with sorrow and regret, "How merciful we should feel when a daughter of the night searches for us." He righted Rosalyn and bowed deeply before her.

He continued, head down, "I should not ask but, please, grace me with your mercy. Tonight, we shall wait. My most deepest apologies, my dear Midnight Maiden. Please accept my humble plea."

Rosalyn's head still spun. She could still feel the wet of his tongue upon her under her chemise. But at least she had until tonight.

"I - I accept," said Rosalyn, hesitant but glad.

The Harlequin stood up and raised a hand to the sky. "To tonight."

"Harley," started Rosalyn but she was quieted by his kiss. Then she became woozy and all became dark.

Chapter 12

"Rosalyn! 'Ey, Rozay," shook Devonté. She laid in her bed bundled up in her covers, back in her normal clothes. She felt phantom kisses on her lips, her neck, her heart, and now her stomach, back and thighs. It was just becoming night.

Devonté had checked the woods for her earlier after he noticed the sun was setting. When he raced back in, fearing the worst, he darted to her room and there he found her, safe and sound. He was so busy unpacking and napping himself, he didn't check on her until night started to fall and everyone noticed she wasn't back yet.

Devonté called downstairs, "She's in her room! She's good!"

Downstairs, Winston asked Demetria over a much-needed cup of coffee in the kitchen, "How'd she get back in without us hearing her?"

Demetria shrugged and leaned against him, wiped out from the vacation. It went half as well as hoped.

Upstairs, Devonté shook Rosalyn more, "C'mon, don't you want to eat?"

Rosalyn felt sluggish and drowsy beyond compare. "Let me sleeeeep," she whined as she shifted deeper into her covers. She didn't want to think about tonight either.

Devonté wanted to shake her more but decided not to. He wanted to put her in his room but figured it would trigger not just a meltdown but a lambasting from his parents about the agreements and stipulations. There were no screams and she was back before nightfall, a deal was a deal. Instead, he just went into his room and set an alarm on his phone to check on her in an hour. Then he just sat at his gaming desk, placed on his headphones and started up a game.

The alarm rang and buzzed as the screen flashed sweeps of color. Devonté turned it off. He noticed the hall was dark; he guessed his parents must have gone to bed early. They were pretty bushed from packing up, driving and unpacking, that was clear.

Devonté paused his game, a solo run on *Star Dust IV*, and pulled on his boots. He pocketed his phone as a precaution. Devonté looked into her room.

She was gone. That wasn't all: the woods glowed gold deep where the river should be.

That's new.

Devonté sped as fast as he could down the stairs and out the house. The gold glow defeated the need for his flashlight, he could see just fine as he darted and dashed through the woods to the river.

The closer he got to the river, the more he saw his sister in her golden chemise, crumpled on the ground. She was bloodied and slashed up as she writhed from her wounds. Ribbons of blood laced her arms and legs, as did deep slashes and tears of flesh. Blots of blood bled through her chemise. She looked towards Devonté with a terrified stare.

She wanted help.

There she laid at the foot of the Harlequin, who smiled cruelly in front of the river. His claws were clean and upwards as he surveyed his work.

Devonté saw Rosalyn slow to a still and close her eyes. He pumped his legs harder — until he couldn't.

As soon as he reached the river clearing, Devonté was lifted off his feet.

"Put me dow—" Devonté's yell was restricted silent by a raised arm of the Harlequin.

The Harlequin broke out into a small titter. "I guess I overdid it a little again," he chuckled. "She was fun but got very boring around the end, as you can see. Tell her this is my last goodbye, my beautiful farewell. She was truly a blessed one of the goddess during all the time I had known her. Such so quaint and gentle — too bad she broke so easy."

Devonté boiled with rage. He fought to speak but all he could muster was a bellowing, *"Why?"*

The Harlequin laughed some more. He cackled deeply under Devonté's hateful stare. Gathering his breath, the Harlequin expressed in the form of an elegant poem:

"I make people see what I want them to see
I make people believe what I want them to believe.
I deceive people when I want to deceive
I let you see because I think it's a little funny
As I play with my beautiful, precious dolly.
My *glorious* Midnight Maiden."

With a regal bow, the Harlequin finished, "I bid you all farewell and a good, gracious night."

And like that, he was gone. The forest was dark. Devonté was dropped. Rosalyn was still not moving.

Devonté scampered to her as he screamed, "No, no, NO!" He gathered up her lifeless body into his lap and cried to the skies, "PLEASE SOMEBODY HELP US!" He took in a deep drag of breath and bellowed as loud as he could, "HELLLLLLLLLP!" His screams eventually crackled into loud sobs.

He sorted through his pockets and dug out his phone to call emergency services.

By the second ring, a woman operator picked up, "New Tulsa emer—"

"My sister is bloody and unconscious! Please, God, just *help us!*" He broke into another terrible sob. He doubled over his sister as he whined out, "Pleeeeease hellllllp. I - I don't— I don't want her to *die!*" Devonté couldn't control his weeping. "Find us!" He ended the call and simply broke down completely as he rocked his sister's body.

The call was sent out quick.

The dispatcher wasn't able to get any details on the injured, if it was caused by violence, details about the caller, or the incident that occurred but they did track the call. It was to a New Tulsan number and located roughly around the suburban house of 3521 Carver Way.

The dispatcher made sure the call asked for a police squad car as well as an ambulance. Given how distressed the caller sounded and how abrupt the phone call ended, it wasn't unreasonable to assume that life was under threat. Especially with the recent visit of invading supremacists. They had been getting driven out in droves by police and sleeper reserve activists but that didn't mean a couple couldn't have darted off to terrorize the neighborhood and frighten the locals. One already was discovered this week trying to enter a school via the gym. The gym teacher happened upon them. As the gym instructor described, the intruder was too busy trying to find the correct door into the school to hear them coming. The teacher already had a metal bat in hand from class and gave the intruder a surprise, bloody home run to the back of the head. Certain the intruder was unconscious, the teacher rang the wall alarm for school lockdown and called the police.

The dispatcher hoped this wouldn't be that. They sent the police along just to be sure.

A squad car and ambulance pulled up and parked on the road in front of the Davis' residence. The police had its lights on but not flashing as it sat in front of the ambulance. The panda colors of the patrol car were maroon and white, reminiscent of the colors on the town's flag. Any lettering on the emergency vehicles were a golden yellow. The ambulance was white with maroon racing stripes on the side. It had a large, bold script on the side that read, "New Tulsa Emergency Services" and "ambulance" in backward letters on the hood. Both vehicles had a maroon Sankofa bird on the right front fender.

The officers were the first to leave their car, tired but stately. All they knew was that there was a possibly violent disturbance that has occurred in this area and possibly at the house they were parked in front of. At least one injured, no other details. But all was quiet around them.

Officer Kelley slammed shut her driver side door with a dark brown hand and said to her partner, Officer Nathan, "You wanna knock or do I?"

Officer Nathan had a toothy smile on his skinny, sable face, "Ladies first."

They both started to the front door as Officer Kelley shook her round head and snickered, "Don't let my wife hear you talkin' like that."

Officer Nathan ribbed back as they both stepped on the stoop and readied themselves in front of the door, "What she gonna do? Tell my husband?"

Officer Kelley took in her last small breath of quiet laughter before she and her partner dropped into police mode with flat, serious faces and she thumped on the door.

"Police and paramedics!" she boomed through the door as her partner radioed his check-in and arrival. He waved at the paramedics backing up on the driveway. The paramedics were seen getting their gear together through the brightly lit backdoor window.

Silence.

Officer Kelley thumped on the door again and even rang the small, brass doorbell to the left of her. Even louder, she boomed, "Police and paramedics!"

Scurrying up behind the two officers was a young, dark-skinned paramedic with round glasses and braids named Donovan with his medical bag in tow. The paramedics got the call that someone was injured but no word on if there was an assailant or not and where they were if so. Donovan hoped there wasn't an assailant and someone just had a vicious slip-and-fall at home. He already had to patch up a supremacist invader handcuffed and tied to the stretcher earlier that week. Two pepperballs to the face and the invader still was lucid enough to say rancid things the police eventually had to gag them for.

Donovan really hoped for a slip and fall.

He gave the cops a bit of a start when he asked right behind them, "Is it safe to come out?"

The officers collected themselves quickly. Officer Nathan explained to Donovan as his partner tried the door one more time, "No bad guy yet but wait for us—"

"May we help you?" asked a bleary Demetria next to her sleepy husband. They felt as if disturbed from a deep and woozy slumber, something that had been striking them on and off over these last few months when they would head to bed. Nothing big to them, they had longtime chalked it up to work. But the lights and sight of the officers cleared them from their drowsiness quicker. It also fell them stunned and silent.

Officer Kelley answered the blank faced parents, "Ma'am, sir, we received a call—"

"PLEASE, GOD, SOMEONE, COME SAVE US!" screeched from the forest out back. "MY SISTER IS *DYING*! GOD, HELLLLLP!"

That was Devonté, both parents thought as they looked over their shoulders into their dark house.

Winston and Demetria hurried the officers and paramedics in and through their home, throwing on any light switches they passed.

Everyone dashed out the house's backdoor into the forest. The officers turned on their shoulder flashlights above their bodycams with a tap as they rushed ahead of the parents into the unfamiliar woods. Their hands were trained above their taser guns on their dominant hand side, right for the both of them. They didn't feel they needed the pistol on their lefts but they also didn't know what they were about to run into and wanted to be prepared. An assailant could still be on the prowl and biding their time for a golden opportunity to attack or flee in these confusing woods.

"Police and paramedics!" both officers bellowed as they hunted down the voice through the forest. Everyone could hear distant male sobbing not too far up ahead.

"Devonté! Rosalyn!" the parents desperately screamed louder than the officers endlessly as they clambered their way through the forest behind the officers.

The paramedic tailed closely behind as he radioed in details on his maroon and yellow walkie talkie — then he bumped into Winston's back.

Everyone stopped when they reached the clearing, paused by what they saw up at the river.

Demetria and Winston's screams rang the night.

Chapter 13

Rosalyn spent days in the hospital — weeks, actually. Bruised and bloody, cracked and worn, she stayed in her hospital bed. Sometimes she labored for breath, sometimes she wept blood. But the Harlequin never came back. Not once. Not ever. Not as a phantom or as a curse. Not as anything. It was over, finally. Off to find a new dolly to break.

And Rosalyn still missed him.

She was brought into New Tulsa Memorial Hospital barely clinging to life. Her dress had to be cut down the center to attend her wounds and revive her. Her family cried as they prayed for her to pull through out in the waiting room. Demetria wailed every time she heard the doctor yell "Clear!" and heard a thump. It happened five times.

When Rosalyn woke and saw the doctors, she screamed for the Harlequin to come back and save her with the ragged whole of her being. Her family could hear her shriek, "What are you doing with my *body*? Harley!

Harlequin! Save me! Get me out of *here!*" The doctors had to sedate Rosalyn so she would stop fighting back and they could continue saving her life.

All her calls for the Harlequin worried the doctors. They were troubled even more when she answered their questions with, "They're mine! The cuts are mine! Harlequin, I'm so sorry! *Please!*" Several times she broke down whimpering, "I wasn't *enough*. I wasn't enough. I got scared ... he loved me, *honest*. I was just *scared*."

Upon hearing such answers, the doctors all decided to have Rosalyn moved to the psych ward once she was stable enough to leave the Intensive Care Unit. When they reported to the parents her answers and what they wanted to do, the parents tearfully agreed. It pained them to see her like this and horrified them to hear what she said from the doctors.

When Rosalyn was shrieking out in the emergency room, Devonté broke away, steeped in anger and regret, towards the vending machines down the hall in the hospital's canteen area. There, he called his best friends with rage-shaking fingers to inform them there was no more joker to rid. He gave an edited version of events, his voice low and strained as he paced by the hospital vending machines so he wouldn't punch one in anger, sorrow and frustration:

"I ... I took care of him. He's not gonna be a problem anymore .... But ... but ... he messed her up *bad*, man. If I *ever* see him again ... on God, man, on *God*, I'm killin' him by any means necessary. I 'on't care what it take, I 'on't care what I *do*, it's gettin' *done*."

In the end, the pacing wasn't enough. When Devonté hung up, he started beating the light maroon wall beside the short row of vending machines as he thundered out tears and swears. When a security guard tried to restrain him, Devonté sank to the ground and barreled out loud sobs. The guard tried to talk calming words to him but Devonté just cried louder.

Winston was the one to find him when he could hear his son's wails. Winston was heading down himself to the vending machines for a snack he had no desire to eat, he just wanted a break away from the sadness for a bit, though it couldn't leave him. Upon hearing his son and seeing him restrained by a guard, he raced to Devonté. He demanded the guard let his son go, perhaps a bit too roughly but he didn't care. Once the guard released Devonté and got up, Winston held his son close to his chest as they sat together on the floor, tears streaming down his own face. Winston kissed Devonté on the head and wanted to praise him but only more tears came.

Wrapped deep in his mourning father's arms, Devonté promised himself that he would visit Rosalyn every day.

That joker wasn't *getting* another chance. Devonté was *sure* of it. He may not know how to stop him, but that wasn't going to keep him from trying.

When Beepz, N0.nonsense and P0p.killa finally arrived a few days later, they all met in the middle of Wonder City. The weather was lovely, and New Tulsa had successfully scrubbed itself clean of the invaders. However, the moment Devonté had laid eyes on his crew, he sank onto their shoulders, riddled with tears and blurry words about his sister.

The outsider trio decided to stay an extra week past Juneteenth.

Devonté had remained true to his oath since the night he made it, he had visited Rosalyn every day. He didn't have a car but he still made it work: he took buses, walked, or rode with his parents. The hospital was mid-town, just a bit of a hike. However, once his best friends visited, Beepz offered to drive to make Devonté's trips easier. It was the least the crew felt they could do to support Devonté and show care to Rosalyn. They were proud of Devonté for handling the problem on his own but were still saddened by how it all ended for Rosalyn. She didn't deserve all of that, the trio felt. Anything Devonté or Rosalyn needed, they gave without question or pause.

With Beepz's car, and the outsider trio's emotional support, Devonté visited on Juneteenth.

On the day of Juneteenth, the hospital décor was covered in Juneteenth flags, except in the psych ward. Some patients were deeply traumatized by various holidays so celebrations were muted on that ward.

Devonté walked down the brown carpeted halls with POp.killa, Beepz, and N0.nonsense in tow. Beepz was of stocky and average stature. He wore a Juneteenth shirt and a Detroit snapback. He had a fleshy face, medium complexion and a picked-out stubby afro. His mustache and beard were bushy but well-trimmed. He kept his eyes on his phone, turned sideways in his hands.

N0.nonsense was taller, with an undercut fade and gold tipped dreads. He was animated in his swagger, and his personality lit up a room. He was almost Beepz's complexion, just a noticeable shade darker. N0.nonsense had a small goatee. He wore a plain white shirt, black shorts and his newest purchase, a maroon Chocobo Sankofa hat. He was tall and with a bit of a belly.

P0p.killa was the skinniest of the outsider trio. He was slightly darker than Beepz and N0.nonsense but definitely a beanpole in comparison. His hair was in neatly parted twists, a fresh new style from the barbershop he visited a couple days ago. He got blue and red beads at the end of his twists for "free". "Free", as in "he traded his phone number with the barber that twisted his hair the moment he picked up there was a hint of interest, in exchange for the beads." He now had a date for next week. He was growing to like New Tulsa *fast*. He wore a shirt covered in comic book covers and walked in bright orange sneakers. He was clean shaven and occasionally peered at Beepz phone.

Devonté wore a black shirt with white embroidered diamonds on the shoulders. The back of his shirt read "New Tulsa, Est. 1922". Beneath the town name bore a quote:

We rise from the Fire
We rise from the Pressure
As Diamonds

The parents planned to visit later in the day. At least one visited every day. If they couldn't get there, they called.

They were at Freedom Square, collecting as many Juneteenth goodies as they could to bring their daughter. When things had finally cooled down enough after Rosalyn's emergency room visit, Devonté gave them an explanation of the Harlequin that sounded as in-line with the doctors as possible: The Harlequin was a story character Rosalyn simply fell too much in love with. The night everyone found them, she simply went past the river and that's how she wound up so cruelly injured. He simply dragged her back to the other side of the river and started shouting for help. Plain. Simple. Hopefully enough.

This alarmed Winston and Demetria deeply. When the doctors wanted to give Rosalyn a full psych evaluation upon moving Rosalyn out of the Intensive Care Unit, the parents agreed passionately, even more than before. They had no idea her flights of fancy had gotten so bad.

When the doctors came back with the suggestion of acute psychosis, Demetria broke down in tears and Winston wasn't soon far after. Together, they decided to let Rosalyn stay inpatient for as long as it would take to make her well. They had the insurance and New Tulsa had the care.

On this summery Juneteenth day, Devonté and his friends made it to the doors of the psych ward. They were wooden double doors with little bird cut outs taped on as a feeble attempt at decor. Devonté tapped the silver button on the intercom, just like he learned to do during his first few trips. It surprised him the psych ward looked like nothing he saw in his games. Nothing was creepy, no padded rooms, no strait jackets. Just a normal hospital wing.

"May I help you?" a male voice crackled through.

Devonté answered, "Uh, it's Devonté Davis. I'm here to see a Rosalyn Davis? Family visit."

"Oh, oh, Devonté," the voice crackled. Devonté visited so much, he almost didn't need to go through the formalities. "We'll send somebody down to let you in."

"Okay, thank you," replied Devonté. He looked behind him and saw everyone huddled around Beepz's phone. "What is y'all watchin—"

"Benlie 'bout to say somethin'!" hushed POp.killa. He beckoned Devonté forth.

It was a livestream of Freedom Square. Freedom Square was completely decked out in Juneteenth decorations. Banners, streamers, live bands, the lot. A long, narrow stage stood behind the fire statue and had an empty podium. On the left of the podium sat the mayor. She was an aged, stately woman with gray dreads wrapped up in a beautiful bouffant and deep brown skin. She had on a shirt donning the town's flag. On the right side sat the chief of police, a broad shouldered, proud man with a mahogany complexion and a round jaw. Above his badge sat several bar strips of many colors but the one bar that stood out most was of the colors of the trans flag. He was proud of who he was for a reason and always strove to keep his town safe with that pride. From a S.T.A.R. during the Stonewall days as a youngster becoming a young man to a chief coming up in his years, he never lost sight of protecting those who lives mattered. New Tulsa's police force didn't start the way most did in the nation. Instead, they were the first and last stand against those who dared for a second try of terror when New Tulsa was a young city and growing safe haven.

A second try never happened.

The town's community leaders and the some of the surviving elders of the Tulsa massacre sat beside the mayor and the chief in padded metal chairs. Some survivors were represented by their offspring.

A stocky woman with skin like the darkest cinnamon walked up to the podium. She had on wired earrings shaped like cowrie shells and her shock mauve braids folded up into a single, raised French braid. Her outfit was eye catching: an all-white suit with a maroon Sankofa bird animated and blinking its single eye on her lapel, as if woven in but alive.

She received cheer, claps and adoration from the crowd. Some even whooped, "Wonder City!", to which Benlie gave a kind laugh, showing her dimples.

Before she could begin, a nurse buzzed the door and asked, "Devonté?"

The boys looked up and followed the nurse, a seasoned young man with tattoos and a kind voice, through the halls and doors as Benlie spoke.

On the mic, Benlie said, "Thank you, home." She grinned kindly to the claps. "This town sure has seen a lot. It started from a lot, too. A lot of pain. A lot of death. A lot of lies from a lot of those who should have told the truth." She paused. "But here we are: Alive." The crowd whooped and clapped. She shrugged, "Just … alive. Having families, working jobs, living fully. That's *all* we ever wanted. All we ever wanted.

"Not to be dragged to unknown lands to be beaten and tortured. Not to be chased in the streets by those who wish us harm. Not to be murdered or terrorized in cold, merciless blood.

"And so ... we did what we do best: We made the best out of the worst. And we *survive*. If there is any constant about us, we're brilliant survivors. And not just survivors. Thrivers. We *live*. We have *lives*.

"It makes them mad, I know. But, hey, I'd be pretty mad too if what I kept trying to crush just. Keeps. *Surviving*. The worst of it, the hell of it, the evil of it. All of it. No wonder why they're mad." Quick cheers for Wonder City spurred from the crowd, Benlie smiled to herself and continued.

"Let them be mad. At least they know one thing for sure: Even with their best shot, even with the cheat codes, it's game over. We're not going *anywhere*. But! But we *will* be moving forward, like always. Thank you and Happy Juneteenth, everybody!" Benlie waved.

The crowd roared as Benlie exited the podium.

"Nice speech," complemented N0.nonsense. The others agree wholeheartedly.

Then Benlie rushed back on stage to the mic, her smile still plastered on her face but with an added furrowed brow. "There ain't no ticket on my Latimer, right? It's just I'm staring at the chief and he had a smile that made me wonder."

The crowd laughed, including the chief.

"I'm just sayin', he runs this town like a clock!" She joked to the chief directly, "I'm not parked nowhere bad, I promise."

The chief waved in laughter and shouted, not aided by a mic, "You're good!"

Benlie pointed to the back and directed as she enjoyed the moment, "'Ey, community centre crew! If you're hearing me, light up the steps in this man's favorite colors. It's June, it's Juneteenth, I want to see some loud and proud!"

The crowd cheered and laughed as Benlie hurried off the mic, patting the chief's shoulder as she passed.

The boys chuckled as they were led to Rosalyn's room.

Usually, anyone who wasn't a doctor or nurse was not allowed in patients' rooms but as Rosalyn was still bed-ridden and a minor, special allowances were made. As long as the door remained open and in view of the nurse's station, all was fine.

The nurse knocked on Rosalyn's open door; she was looking out of the picture window over the city and the sea. She still had her necklace. Her gold headdress had long faded away as it sat in a medium, clear plastic hospital bag behind the nurse's station in the Patients' Belongings room. Her dress was discarded after it was cut off to save her life. It, too, faded away in the bin when the lights were off and darkness swallowed the room. She missed her chemise. She was allowed to keep her necklace, to keep most of her meltdowns at bay. The parents okayed it. They wanted her as comfortable as possible.

"Rosalyn?" asked the nurse. He hoped she was chatty today, he had always found her reserved and quiet. He would have offered her books but those were restricted for the time being. He noticed she wasn't much for TV and even less for games of any sort. Instead, he saw she preferred to stay by the window and stare, unless she had a visitor.

Rosalyn looked towards the door. Her face was healing. The smaller cuts were little, thin traces of scars tracked about. The bigger slashes by her neck and on her cheek were covered with glossy, white sheets of gauze and still needed to be monitored closely. But they were all healing, all the same. Her legs had terrible gashes, as if someone hacked at her with scythes and sickles. No sign of any sexual assault or worse, the doctors checked, but plenty of signs that the doctors summed up as vicious self-harm, especially since Rosalyn claimed she did it to herself for her "Harlequin".

The doctors noted she couldn't walk. Though they soon learned from her many meltdowns she could certainly kick, and fairly hard at that, but she needed a wheelchair to get around. When prompted to walk, Rosalyn simply couldn't. Her legs shook and collapsed too much when she was upon them. She couldn't stop sobbing either, riddled with apologies and teary promises to her "Harlequin". The doctors figured the walking problem was psychosomatic. She just needed time and therapy, both mental and physical.

At his sister's door, Devonté asked for everyone to wait outside with a gesture and entered. The nurse walked off to attend to other things but the outsider trio crowded together with supportive smiles and little hellos.

Carefully and kindly, Devonté approached Rosalyn. "Hey, Rozay."

She smiled at him. He visited her all the time but she never tired of it.

Devonté sat on her bed. The glint of her necklace caught his eye. Every time he saw that necklace, he wanted to rip it off and throw it into the sea.

He smiled, "How're you feelin'? I brought the boys around." He gestured to the door, where his friends waved from the doorway.

Rosalyn found Devonté's friends nurturing in their care of her, during her stay. They always asked how she fared, and they always attempted to lighten her mood with jokes and silly, cute memes and pictures they found across the internet. She knew they meant well, they cared for her like their own little sister, spearheaded by her big brother. Actually, her hospital stay was her first time meeting them. She only knew of them as names Devonté floated about during his retellings of his gaming escapades or when he chatted to them during raids. They charmed her with their joviality and infectious mirth but she still missed her Harlequin.

Rosalyn waved back to them with polite delicateness and answered, "I'm okay." She picked at her nails with her partly buzzy-numb fingers and asked quieter to her brother, "Have..."

"Rosie, please let him go," Devonté softly urged. He tried to hide the concern on his face so his friends wouldn't see. She asked the same thing every visit. "He said it himself, he's gone. *Gone*, Rose."

Tears beaded up in Rosalyn's eyes. Every night, she would wish to the sky for his return. For another caress, another phantom kiss—

"Rose, you got to move on. Please," begged Devonté, his voice low.

Beepz saw Devonté's concerned body language, the worried look that slipped onto his face.

"Hey," said Beepz to the duo, "let's sit down somewhere."

Reading the situation, the other two complied and all three of the young men sought out an empty table in the ward's eating area. They could tell this was going to be another heavy one, as some visits were. The trio decided to watch the rest of the Juneteeth livestream with the volume on low and wait for Devonté to call them in.

Devonté noticed everyone left the door to give him privacy. He continued, "Why can't you see that you are already enough? Why?" Tears gathered in his eyes. He tried to blink them back but a couple fell. Water crept into his voice a little, "Why, do …. Do you know what I *saw*? When I found you? When … when you were reaching out?" He sniffed. "I - I could tell you wanted to go *home*."

Rosalyn turned her head away. When she had met the Harlequin that night, she tried to let him undress her and be passionate with her again but she simply couldn't go through with it and he knew it. When she attempted to guide his caressing hand back up her thigh and hip to her arm instead, that's when the slashes and rage began. She never thought she could scream so hard before. Nor feel so much pain. Last she remembered was seeing Devonté run to her from so far away. And then, nothing.

Her tears dropped onto her bandaged forearms. The bandages hid the several gashes on her arms. She was going to need surgery for all the nerve damage she sustained. She could barely hold a pencil now. Rosalyn wiped her eyes with the back of her hands, dotted with more bandages.

Her lips trembled as she talked, "He ... he was everything to me. E-everything." Rosalyn broke down into her hands.

Devonté hugged her. He, too, started to cry as he pressed into her shoulder. He rarely had a visit where he remained dry-eyed the entire way through.

"Please know that you're already enough," whispered Devonté.

Rosalyn cried a little harder. She had never really seen herself as much of anything. She loved her stories because they always made her feel like she was more. Something outstanding, noteworthy, *amazing*. She could live through the characters and become someone she felt she never was. Someone confident. Someone boisterous. Someone ... interesting.

"I love you more than you will *ever* know," quaked Devonté. "I won't leave you. I won't abandon you. I just want you to be there for *you*."

"I - I know," sniffed Rosalyn.

"Then *please* be there for you. Please," begged Devonté "I'll always have your back but I need *you*." He sniffed harder, "I need you to be *there* for *you*."

Rosalyn wished she could but didn't know how. All she knew was that she simply had a long road ahead of her.

She kissed her brother's cheek and wept on his shoulder.

Other works

Null(Void)

In Search of Amika

Dreamer

Kinetics

The Glassman

Stalwart

About the Author

MultiMind lives in Baltimore, Maryland. She tries to find time for her countless hobbies, from 3D printing to bookbinding to virtual reality. She writes books that are fairly Black, usually queer, and very much embedded in the world of Sci-Fi, Fantasy & Horror.